OLIVER
NOCTURNE

OLIVER NOCTURNE

THE VAMPIRE'S PHOTOGRAPH

KEVIN EMERSON

SCHOLASTIC INC.

NEW YORK   TORONTO   LONDON   AUCKLAND   SYDNEY
MEXICO CITY   NEW DELHI   HONG KONG   BUENOS AIRES

For A.E., C.M. and H.M-A, my first readers . . .

No part of this publication may be reproduced, stored in a retrieval system, or transmitted in any form or by any means, electronic, mechanical, photocopying, recording, or otherwise, without written permission of the publisher. For information regarding permission, write to Scholastic Inc., Attention: Permissions Department, 557 Broadway, New York, NY 10012.

ISBN-13: 978-0-545-05801-8
ISBN-10: 0-545-05801-5

12 11 10 9 8 7 6 5 4 3 2   9 10 11 12 13/0

Printed in the U.S.A.   40
First printing, August 2008

Contents

Prologue

At the center of everything, stood a Gate.

The Gate had never been opened. It had been made, and then shut. Some said that the sound of it closing began the universe. No one knew what was on the other side of it. Nor did anyone know what would happen if the Gate was opened. No one was even completely sure what the Gate did, yet all agreed that it was very important, maybe the most important thing in the universe. Why it was important, though, was the subject of a debate as old as the Gate itself.

Most believed that the Gate was not meant to be opened — that keeping it closed was the point of everything. They believed that opening it would end the universe, by unhinging the many worlds and sending them crashing down on one another. Those who believed this were also usually the ones who found the universe to be tolerable the way it was. And they had it easy. Since the Gate seemed to be forever shut, few of them were worried.

But others wondered: Why make a *gate*? Why not just a wall? Wasn't a gate meant to be opened? Thus, they believed that opening the Gate was the point of everything. That if it was opened, the universe would finally *begin,* and all of the unfair suffering would end. Those who believed this were also usually the ones who were suffering, whether at the hands of ruthless leaders, backward societies, or fate.

Yet they had been very busy. They had tried many times to open the Gate and failed, but doing what seemed to be impossible required a great deal of learning, perseverance, and vigilance. So, they studied the signs and oracles, and waited.

Until it was finally time to try again.

For the first time in a span longer than anyone could rightly measure, someone approached the Gate. He came on the only road. The first sound to reach the Gate was that of wooden wheels grinding on crushed volcanic glass. The wheels halted. A black stagecoach had arrived. From it stepped a tall man in a crisp, pin-striped suit. He wore a bow tie and a fedora hat, and looked as if he'd just left a respectable banking institution. His eyes, while wizened and old, were surrounded by the face of a young man, his features as clean and crisp as his hat and suit. He certainly did not bear the wear and tear one would expect after the long journey to Nexia, the center world of the universe, where the Gate stood.

The gentleman surveyed its striking bronze form, which shone brightly against a backdrop of pure black and starlight. There was no atmosphere in Nexia, and so the tight clusters of galaxies, novas, and planets sparkled in the dark like glass ornaments, seeming to hang almost within reach. Rings of dust and solar flare arced overhead. Wormholes spiraled away into the black.

The gentleman looked off to either side of the Gate. Ripples of blood-red land spread away to the horizon. Marble columns and spires of jade and amethyst stuck out of the red rock here and there, as if the ground had frozen in mid-stir. There had once been a civilization here, in a time before anyone could remember. Some believed that it was this civilization that had created the Gate, then departed through it. Some even called these people the Architects. Those who sought to open the Gate also wanted to ask the Architects a few questions, ideally at the point of a deadly instrument.

The gentleman turned to the two zombie horses that had borne his coach here and gave them a slap, which sent them away. He watched them go, the stagecoach clattering behind them, until there was only silence, then he turned and walked toward the Gate. He stopped just inside its brilliant aura and bowed deeply, with a respectful tip of his hat.

Thirty years passed.

Then the Gate spoke in the gentleman's mind, *Why come ye?*

The gentleman smiled. *I mean to open you,* he thought back.

And who are ye who comes? the Gate asked.

I am Illisius, he replied.

I see, said the Gate.

Illisius put down his briefcase and sat, cross-legged, on the road.

Another twenty years went by.

You are patient, for a demon, the Gate observed.

I am waiting for someone, Illisius said. Then he pushed back his finely pressed cuff and checked his silver watch. Seven dials spun at different speeds. *He'll be here soon.*

Ah, yes, the Gate agreed. *The young vampire.*

Illisius nodded.

Silence resumed. Overhead, a wormhole siphoned off the debris of one of Nexia's rings, spun it into a planet, and sent it away. Later, there was a pop, as one overwhelmed world cleaved in two.

In the shadow of Nexia's Gate, Illisius waited.

CHAPTER 1

The Intruder in the Mirror

Oliver Nocturne had been having trouble sleeping, which was why he first heard the intruder. He had been lying awake as usual one November morning, tossing and turning, when a floorboard had creaked somewhere upstairs. Going to investigate had seemed much more interesting than lying in bed with the thoughts that plagued him. Now, it was December, and the intruder was back for the third time. So far, Oliver was the only member of his family who knew.

Oliver had been having trouble sleeping for as long as he could remember. It had always been particularly bad around his birthday and Christmas, both of which were coming right up, but this year it was worse than ever. He was lying awake well into each day and waking up exhausted each evening. Oliver was bothered most by one thought in particular: *There's something wrong with me.* The problem was, Oliver didn't know what that *something* was. He just knew that he didn't quite fit in with those around him, neither at home or at school. Oliver kept this feeling to himself, mainly because he was embarrassed. Vampires weren't supposed to have these kinds of problems. And if his older brother, Bane, ever found out, well, there would be no end to the torment.

The one thing that Oliver did know about his problem was that it seemed to be about his future. Oliver was thirteen in human years, which meant that it wouldn't be too long now before he received his demon. But that happened to every young vampire, and most kids looked forward to growing up. Kids at school talked about it like it was the greatest thing. What kind of vampire wouldn't want to get his demon? To be able to do the things adult vampires did, like occupy animals and go out on the Friday hunt? So there had to be something *else* about the future that was keeping him up day after day. Sometimes, he almost felt like he knew what it was . . . yet he could never quite put his finger on it. He would chase his thoughts around, one, then the next, always feeling like some truth was just beyond his reach.

This morning, though, his awful insomnia had brought something interesting: The intruder was back. Oliver could hear footsteps echoing from upstairs. He quietly slipped out of his coffin and down to the stone floor. The underground crypt was silent, lit only by a faint crimson glow. Oliver's parents, Phlox and Sebastian, were asleep together in a wide coffin beside his. Bane's coffin was over by the wall, also shut tight. Oliver had heard his parents go to bed hours ago and heard Bane sneaking in after that.

He crossed the room and started up a stone spiral staircase, leaving the crypt, which was the lowest level of his family's underground home. His bare feet padded lightly on the stones, the slight ruffling of his pajamas the only other sound. The lanterns on the walls, teardrop-shaped crystal globes sitting in ornate lead sconces, had been drained of their magmalight for the day, so the staircase was pitch-black, but that was no problem for vampire eyes. He reached the main floor, where he peered into the dark kitchen. The titanium appliances hummed softly. Another footstep sounded above.

Oliver continued up the stairs, which ended on the next landing. In front of him was a sleek steel door. He put his ear to it and heard more creaking steps from the other side. Technically, he wasn't allowed up here. . . . But Oliver pressed a red button, and the door slid silently open.

There was a narrow space, and then the back of a broken, rusted refrigerator. It was leaning at an angle against the wall, wires and coils hanging from it as if it was a great beast that had been clawed open. Oliver squeezed around the side of it —

And saw the human.

A girl was standing in the center of a large room. This was the ground floor of the abandoned house that sat atop Oliver's home. The walls that had once separated the rooms of the house had been torn away, leaving a long, vacant space cluttered with rubble. The whole place was supposed to look run-down and unsafe. Phlox had taken great care to make it feel not only neglected, but forbidding — homeless people *could* sleep here, but why would they want to? A gang of kids *could* hang out here, but wasn't there maybe a cooler place to go?

Two beams of gloomy Seattle morning light angled in, through broken windows on either side of the front door. Dark burgundy wallpaper sagged from the walls, revealing pocked plaster and blooms of mold. A giant hole gaped just in front of the door. It wasn't a real hole but a design trick Phlox had perfected. The girl hadn't used the door, though. She always came in through the window, using a set of thick plaid oven mitts to navigate the window's toothlike shards of broken glass.

She stood now, mitts under her arm, silently survey-ing the room's contents. There was much to look at: In addition to the peeling wallpaper and bottomless hole, there was an ancient bathtub in the corner, full of putrid water and reeking of rot. A slow, steady drip plinked into it from the sagging ceiling, where a broken chandelier hung cockeyed. In the other corner was an overturned dresser, its filthy clothes strewn into the brown puddles on the floor.

On the wall above the dresser hung a dingy painting in a tarnished, cracked frame. It was a portrait of a wiry, dour old man in a tweed suit, with very little hair, and if one looked closely, even less skin. But these details were obscured by mold. His piercing eyes however, which seemed to glow with an unnatural amber light, remained bright; again, part of Phlox's intention when designing the room. The picture was of Oliver's departed great-uncle, Renfeld.

And yet, of all these unsettling things, each time the girl came, she spent the most time looking at the one thing that, as Sebastian had once explained to Oliver, no human could resist — the tall mirror leaning against the far wall, directly opposite Oliver's perch behind the refrigerator. Dad had said that humans loved seeing themselves in a mirror, *preferred* it, actually. A mirror would captivate a human like a moth to a flame. The girl stood in front of it now, having no idea that Oliver was watching her, because he had no reflection. Even if he'd had one, it would have been hard to see. The glass was covered with a thick film of grime, except for one circular area. The girl had cleaned this spot on her first visit. She reached up now and wiped the circle again with her cuff.

She was slightly shorter than him, wearing jeans, the

same green puffy vest and maroon knit hat that she always wore, and, today, a turtleneck sweater with bright stripes that stood out strikingly against the drab world around her. She stood with her hands on her hips, turning this way and that, every now and then reaching up and flicking at her thick braid of brown hair. She made a silly face in the mirror, baring her soft, rounded human teeth and holding up her stubby human fingers as if they were claws. She almost laughed, but then sighed and slumped her shoulders.

As Oliver watched her, he felt a wave of guilt. He should have told his parents about the girl after her first visit. He had planned to, but now she'd visited more than once and Oliver would end up getting in trouble, too. Phlox and Sebastian would want to know why he hadn't told them immediately, and what would his answer be? That he'd been curious about what she was up to and wanted to figure out why she kept coming here? What kind of a vampire would have a thought like that? Bane would have more of a field day with this than with Oliver's insomnia. There was also the possibility that Oliver's parents would decide that this trespassing needed to be stopped in a more permanent way, and then Oliver would have nothing to distract him from his sleeplessness. Besides, this girl was harmless, wasn't she? All she ever did was come here, look around for a while, then leave —

Only now she did something different. She reached into her vest and pulled out a large black object that hung from her neck on a faded leather strap. It took Oliver a moment to recognize that it was a camera. He'd learned about it in school, a device that a human used to capture an image. Vampires never used cameras. They painted portraits in oil or drew sketches in charcoal. In fact, Oliver's parents had told him to avoid ever having his picture taken, but he wasn't sure why. It couldn't hurt him, like sunlight or a stake, at least as far as he knew.

The girl held the camera to her eye, slowly twisting the lens to focus, then pressed a button. There was a click. She wound a small lever and looked through it again.

Oliver watched her turn slowly about, the camera clicking. Why would she be taking pictures of *this* place? Oliver's family had lived here on Twilight Lane since he was very young. It was one of the streets in town where almost every house looked abandoned and run-down on the surface, yet had a vampire home beneath it. These houses were never condemned or torn down, because Sebastian's employer, the Half-Light Consortium, had vampires working undercover in important human jobs for the city. Whenever someone in the human public called for tearing down the decrepit houses on Twilight Lane, some permit or legal document would get fouled up somewhere and set the process off by years. It was in ways like this that the vampires had built a society right under the humans' noses. Sebastian said it hadn't been that hard, because humans were very good at not noticing things that were right in front of them. He also said that the biggest reason why humans didn't know about the vampires was that they didn't really *want* to know.

But this girl seemed pretty curious. Maybe she just liked cold, abandoned places. That would be weird for a human, but interesting. As she continued snapping photos, Oliver slipped out from behind the refrigerator and stepped to the wall. Putting both hands against the damp plaster, he took a deep, meditative breath. . . . A trace of whispers brushed across his mind, speaking in ancient vampire tongues. He felt a lightening in his feet and proceeded to scale the wall like a spider. He'd only recently begun learning how to work with the forces. Climbing walls was one of the early skills: a prelude to levitation. Vampires could do these things because they could sense forces from other worlds. From their very first years in school, vampires were taught that this world was only one of many, most of which weren't so frustratingly physical and mortal. Each world had its own set of dimensions and rules: some very similar to Earth, some very different. The forces of nearby worlds mingled through one another, and while humans couldn't sense them, vampires could. As Oliver's teachers always put it, this was one of the many advantages that the undead had over the living.

When Oliver reached the top of the wall, he paused, concentrated further, then slid up onto the ceiling. He crawled slowly forward around the frayed rope that held the broken chandelier, until he was right above the girl. Now he could hear her breathing. It was a strange sound, so frail. Like it could stop at any time. Also, from this close, he could vividly smell her. Humans barely had any idea that they had a scent but, to a sensitive vampire nose, it was an all-in-one guide to their attitudes, hopes, and fears. In past visits, Oliver had sensed that this girl was frustrated, and that there was some sadness beneath this frustration. Tonight, though, she was focused on what she was doing. She loved taking pictures. But she was nervous, too. Oliver could feel her pulse racing.

The girl took a step, and now she was just a little ahead of him. As she aimed the camera at the broken refrigerator, Oliver concentrated hard and let go with his hands, hanging down from his knees. His head ended up just a few inches behind the girl's shoulder. He wanted to see the room as she was seeing it, albeit upside down. Then he noticed her teardrop-shaped silver earring and reached for it. He didn't think about what he was doing — it was second nature to vampires to collect artifacts and trinkets that interested them. It seemed like the natural thing to do. He had just started to gently pull the earring free from her earlobe —

"Ahh!" she cried out, flinching. Oliver flashed back up to the ceiling. The girl's hand zipped through the space he'd just occupied, flicking at her own ear, and knocking off the earring. It fell into a moldy crack in the floor. The girl whipped her head around. Oliver flattened himself, his back against the plaster, arms and legs out.

Now a boy's voice whisper-shouted from outside. "Emalie! Are you all right?" She had never brought anyone else along before.

"Yes," the girl — Emalie — replied. She sounded scared, but also embarrassed.

"What happened?"

"Nothing!" Emalie kept looking around the room. "Stupid spiders," she muttered.

And then her body froze, her breath catching in her throat, and she began to turn her head upward.

Oliver leaned back against the ceiling. He reached out through the forces and began to fade out of sight. Those who were true masters of spectralization could disappear completely. They literally sent their matter into a parallel world, existed as a spirit for a short while, then gathered back their solid form. Oliver had just started learning this skill, so the best he could do was make himself into little more than a shadow. Hopefully in this gloom, that would be enough.

Emalie's eyes reached the ceiling. She looked right at Oliver.

Then she shook her head and looked away. She felt at her ear. "Shoot," she said, discovering that her earring was missing. She looked down at the grimy floor and kicked at a lump of moldy clothing.

Oliver relaxed and reappeared above her. There was no chance she'd find that earring. He could barely see it.

The boy called again from outside. "We're going to be late!"

"Dean! Hold on —" Emalie said.

Oliver heard Dean huff outside.

Emalie gave up looking for the earring, then pulled another large contraption from her vest and affixed it to the top of the camera — a flash. She peered into the eyepiece, twisted the lens, then depressed a button. The flash exploded, filling the room with blinding light. Oliver winced, feeling as if his eyes had been stretched too wide. He blinked over and over, brilliant green obscuring his view. The girl aimed the camera at the dresser. She focused. This time Oliver squinted, but the flash seared his vision anyway.

Despite the green blobs in his eyes, he hung down behind her again and watched, fascinated, as she documented the whole room. It was lucky that she was using such an old camera. Because she had to look through an eyepiece, the view that she'd see would be bounced off a tiny mirror, and so even if she aimed the camera right at him, Oliver would be invisible to her. Still, he didn't plan on letting that happen —

Then, Emalie took a step back, and Oliver almost didn't move in time. He shot back up to the ceiling, scrambling to her left as he did so. He just avoided her, but his foot caught the rope holding the chandelier. There was a shrill clinking of glass —

Emalie spun around again, camera still to her eye, aiming right at him before he could react.

The flash exploded with light.

"Tsss!" Oliver threw an arm across his eyes. He tried to keep his concentration, to hang on to the forces, but he was losing his hold. His feet began to slip off the ceiling, and he hurled himself blindly away. He arced across the room, slammed into the far wall, and fell straight into the bathtub with a tremendous splash.

Oliver hit the bottom hard and stayed there, panicked, as the water sloshed about. Once it calmed, he could see Emalie frozen in place, her eyes darting from the tub to the ceiling and around the room.

"I . . . is someone there?" she asked the empty room, her voice trembling.

Stay still, Oliver thought. He watched from the safety of the dark, murky water as Emalie backed slowly toward the window, tucking her camera into her vest. Since he didn't need to breathe, he could stay in this tub all day, though it was unpleasantly cold.

"Emalie!" he heard Dean call again. She slipped on her oven mitts and, when her back bumped into the wall, she turned and scrambled out, carelessly knocking shards of glass this way and that. "Ow!" she cried out as the knee of her jeans ripped.

Oliver slowly slipped out of the tub and moved across the room, leaving sopping footprints on the floor, until he reached the edge of the gray daylight. Even on a gloomy, misting morning such as this, the light made him squint. At the bottom of the wildly overgrown, spiderweb-laced lawn, he saw Dean standing in a narrow gap in the high hedge that surrounded the Nocturnes' house. He was tall, with two backpacks hanging off his lanky frame like he was a coat rack. Even from this distance, Oliver could smell the uncertainty — and worry — that Dean was feeling. Emalie reached him, and Dean handed over one of the bags. He immediately disappeared up the street, but Emalie glanced warily toward the house.

Oliver leaned back into the shadows. When he looked again, she was gone. He stepped to the side of the window, where he could see the busy intersection at the end of Twilight Lane. Emalie and Dean had reached the corner.

"What happened in there?" Oliver heard Dean ask.

"Nothing," Emalie said between heavy breaths. "Come on, already." Emalie grabbed his arm and dragged him into the street, even though the signal said DON'T WALK.

"Emalie —" Dean's whining was lost in the churning of engines and splashing tires.

Lines of cars sped by, spraying water. Emalie's striped sweater stood out against the wet gray world, like it was the only object that had been colored in. Oliver watched until they disappeared behind the traffic.

He returned to the area where Emalie had been standing. It took a moment, but he located the earring and fished it out of the crack in the floor. Then he slipped quietly back downstairs, into dry clothes, and into his coffin. He was asleep in moments.

CHAPTER 2

A Breakfast of Lies

When Oliver's alarm went off the next evening, he barely heard it. Rolling over, he slapped it off and shut his eyes.

Suddenly, the lid of his coffin was flying open. "Oliver!" He rolled over to find his mother, Phlox, looming over him, arms crossed. She was up and dressed early as usual, her long platinum hair tied back. She wore a fashionable black shirt and pants, with a burgundy apron tied around her waist and a livid scowl on her face.

Oh, no, Oliver thought miserably. *She knows about Emalie.*

But then Phlox continued, "You're half an hour late!" She reached down and began yanking him out of bed. Soil, which vampires used like blankets, scattered onto the floor. "You can clean that up later," Phlox began.

"Come on, Mom!" Oliver's tone of voice surprised even himself, and his normally brown eyes flared with an amber glow. He jerked his arm away from her and trudged toward the large ebony armoire. He knew he had no right to be annoyed, *he* was the one who was late, but still . . .

"Tssss!" Suddenly, Phlox vaulted through the air, landing in front of him, her pearl white teeth clenched and bared. She hissed and grabbed him by both shoulders, her hazel eyes glowing turquoise. When she spoke, her voice was low and frigid. "Excuse me?"

Oliver was shocked, not by the force of Phlox's grip or the anger on her face — those were not unusual for vampires — but by his own attitude. He wanted to snap, *Get off me!* But luckily, he kept that rebellious voice to himself. He didn't want to make things worse, especially when he was lucky that Phlox was only mad at him about being late. "Sorry." He sulked.

Phlox's face immediately softened, and the glow faded from her eyes. The next second, she was ruffling Oliver's hair. "Hurry upstairs. Even your brother is up." Oliver nodded, and Phlox swept out of the room.

Oliver dressed in his school uniform: pressed black pants, a white button-down shirt, and a tie. He threw on a dark gray sweatshirt and sneakers and hurried up to the kitchen.

The staircase lanterns were now filled with molten, golden magmalight, which swirled with bits of cinder and gave off a warm glow. The kitchen was lit by tiny spotlight globes on the ceiling. These burned hotter and brighter, closer to a pure white. The Nocturnes' entire house was lit by magmalight, which was harnessed from deep within the mantle of the earth. In addition, its pipes ran through the walls and floors, keeping the house heated to a perfect 98.6 degrees.

Oliver sat on a stool at the center island. Bane glanced up from across the island with exhausted eyes, then hunched back over his breakfast of blood angel cake and coffee. His shaggy black hair hung down in his eyes, a dyed-red shock shooting down the middle. Since Bane was a vampire with a demon, as all high school students were, he no longer had to worry about a dress code. He wore a ratty T-shirt over a white long underwear top with the cuffs torn off. His jeans, held up only somewhat by a studded belt, were rolled above high black work boots, which were tied with thin chain laces.

Phlox immediately turned around with a still-sizzling slice of the fried red cake. She slid it across the island to Oliver, along with a Coke and a vitamin-size capsule of crushed herbs. Oliver dug into the sugary cake. It was not a normal breakfast in the ancient tradition, but Oliver and his family were New World vampires and embraced a modern way of living.

There were, of course, Old World vampires, like Oliver's grandparents. They lived in Morosia, one of the many Underworld cities beneath Europe and Asia, and they disapproved of almost everything about the New World vampires' way of life. They thought it was too *human* and they never let Phlox and Sebastian hear the end of it. Like most adult arguments, the debate between the New World and the Old World often sounded to Oliver like two sides of the same coin. No vampires wanted to be human. In fact, all vampires, if they had their choice, would much rather have been living in another world altogether, where they could roam free without always worrying about being killed by sunlight or stakes, but that wasn't possible. Vampires were trapped on Earth.

The only part of Phlox and Sebastian's New World life that the grandparents couldn't complain about was the very thing that made them grandparents: New World vampires had discovered how to have children. It used to be that there were only adult vampires. Phlox and Sebastian had been sired. They had been humans in their late teens when they were bitten and turned into vampires. Vampires had always wanted families — love was not just an emotion felt by the living and the good — but human children couldn't be successfully sired. Their bodies were too fragile and their spirits too pure. Yet while Old World vampires continued to sire young adults, New World alchemists had discovered how to create children by combining the DNA of two parents, in a process that used the human science of genetics and multi-world physics. New World children were grown in a special lab until they were old enough to be "born," meaning that they were removed from their vessels and brought home by their parents. Even Phlox's and Sebastian's snarly old parents had to admit: They loved their grandchildren.

Having kids forever changed the way of life for New World vampires, especially when they discovered that their new children did not have demons. An adult vampire was the combination of a human body and a demon spirit, which came from one of the other worlds. But just as a human child could not survive being sired, a vampire child's mind and body were not ready to be inhabited by a demon. Only when vampire children had grown enough, learned enough, and become strong enough would they receive their demons and become adults.

Vampire children were also not strong enough to drink the blood of humans. While adult vampires could survive on human blood and nothing else, nourished by its potent life forces, New World children needed an entirely different diet. Above all else, they needed sugar to feed their brains. So, a diet high in white flour and processed sugars that could easily be converted to glucose was ideal. Cakes and confections were now the staple foods at vampire family meals. Even the adults would indulge in eating them, the difference being that *their* accompanying goblet would be of human blood, while a child's goblet would contain blood from one of the less potent creatures, such as pig, wolf, ostrich, or even bear. Each kind of blood brought with it different aspects of life force and mineral content. Variety was a key to proper growth and development. Iguana, bat, or kitten blood was especially high in antibacterial agents, which helped keep away troublesome conditions that the undead had to deal with, like decay and rot.

The breakfast Oliver now ate, blood angel cake, was very popular: a sweet angel food cake that was marinated to a deep crimson color and then fried.

"Did you sleep any better?" Phlox asked.

Oliver shoved a big bite in his mouth, then nodded. "Mmm." He felt a wave of relief when Phlox smiled and turned back to her cooking without asking further questions.

A long plasma screen hung above the stone counter. Phlox had it tuned to a cable news weather report. A weatherman in a trench coat was standing outside in a gale-force wind. His hair was perfect. Behind him, rain flew sideways, and palm trees were bent almost to the ground. "The entire southern coast is absolutely in tatters," he said seriously, yet with a trace of a smirk. "So far five deaths have been attributed to this storm." Below, his name was printed onscreen: KEN TEMPEST,

METEOROLOGIST. The report cut to a house being torn apart by the hurricane winds. Oliver watched with interest. Ken was a household favorite, since, unbeknownst to his television employers, he was a vampire. And he always got the most exciting scoop on the biggest storm tragedies. He even had his own popular video series, entitled *Fatal Storms!* And the fact that it was also a huge seller in the human world was a topic of much humor among vampires.

While Oliver and Bane ate, Phlox busied herself with organizing the refrigerator, which stretched along the top of the wall, above the screen. Its sleek door swung upward to the ceiling with a hiss, revealing racks of hanging blood bags. Phlox kept them meticulously organized by animal and date. Nothing symbolized the Nocturnes' New World vampire culture more than the rows of predrained, free-range, organic blood. Oliver's grandparents, if they could ever have been convinced to visit Seattle, would have gone into a demonic rage at seeing this, ranting about how Phlox and Sebastian were living an anti-*vampyr* life. Old World vampires acted like they would have been quite happy to burn the world to the ground if they could.

Sebastian swept into the room, dressed in a fine suit, long black coat trailing behind him. He was tall and broad, more so than Oliver could ever see himself becoming and, when he was dressed for the office, he embodied all the New World vampire success and refinement. He had been promoted recently to a senior attorney at the Half-Light Consortium, but even before that he had always dressed up, from cuff links to glossy shoes. Sebastian worked so many hours these days, Oliver had trouble picturing him in clothing other than his suits.

He rubbed Oliver's head as he passed. "Hey, Ollie."

"Hi," Oliver responded, but immediately tensed up inside.

"Charles," Sebastian said as he passed Oliver's brother.

"It's *Bane*, Dad," Bane muttered, finishing his breakfast.

"Maybe with your friends," Phlox countered, "but in this house, we'd prefer to use the name we gave you."

"Charles," Bane spat. "It makes me sound like the little *lamb* over there." He cast a scowl at Oliver.

Oliver just kept eating. This was the usual with Bane.

"I'd watch yourself, Charles," Sebastian warned. "And I don't remember hearing you come in this morning."

"So?"

"So" — Phlox's voice lowered — "the other thing you will do while you live in this house is come home on time."

Now Bane almost smiled. "Ty and I got hung up in the park. We found a little human out on his own."

"I see," Sebastian said. He picked up a heavy lead pitcher from the counter and filled a nearby goblet, then turned back to Bane. "So," he continued, sounding reluctantly curious. "How did that go?"

"Oh, man." Bane's sulk immediately gave way to excitement as he recounted his vampire activities.

Oliver watched his parents listening intently to the story, their frustration with Bane forgotten for now. As Bane described his night, Sebastian's eyes lit with a hint of pride. Bane may have been a late-bloomer, having not received his demon until well into high school, and that may have made him a bit rebellious (rebellious in vampire terms being roughly equal to very dangerous in human terms), but really, as long as he graduated, there were worse ways a vampire could turn out.

Like you, little lamb, Oliver thought, hearing Bane's mocking tone in his head. He wondered if he would ever please his parents like Bane did. It didn't seem possible.

Bane finished his story and left the table. Oliver took his last bite of cake, then looked up to find Sebastian staring at him oddly.

"Nothing," Oliver said guiltily, even though his dad hadn't asked him anything.

"You look tired," Sebastian said with a sigh. "We should talk. I've been so busy at work —"

"Dad, I'm fine," Oliver lied.

"You don't look fine. Mom says you're having trouble sleeping." Sebastian raised an eyebrow hopefully. "Is it the dreams?"

"I guess," Oliver lied again. His dad was referring to the dreams that a young vampire had when his demon was coming. A vampire first met his demon in dreams, getting to know the demon's long history, as the demon slowly added his memory and experiences to the vampire's brain. The process was called cohesion. The dreams sometimes came for years before the demon arrived, and they were supposed to be cool — a demon's life was full of violent history. Oliver would have gladly been asleep and having those dreams, rather than lying awake each night like he had been. Still, it seemed easier just to lie to Sebastian.

"Well," Sebastian said, "your yearly doctor's checkup is in a couple days. That always makes you feel better. And the dreams are exciting, aren't they?"

Now Oliver noticed Phlox looking at him as well. Her eyes were wet with tears. Oliver found himself nodding, cementing the lie.

"My baby's growing up. . . ." Phlox smiled. "And so fast." She moved over to Sebastian and put an arm around his waist. "This is much sooner than Charles."

"Mmm," Sebastian agreed. "Sounds fine to me."

Phlox sighed. "Oliver, this is so exciting."

Oliver thought he might explode. How had this happened? Here he was, now with a secret about a human *and* a lie about his demon!

Sebastian leaned over and kissed Phlox. "I have to run."

"Don't forget," Phlox called as he started down the stairs, "I have a committee meeting tonight down at the Central Council."

Sebastian nodded, but his brow furrowed. "I'll try not to be too late." He disappeared back down the stairs, heading for their main door to the sewers below.

Oliver started to turn away from the table. "Don't forget to take your vitamins," Phlox said as she resumed her organizing.

"Right." Oliver nodded, but inside he scowled. The capsule, full of a crushed blend of dark herbs, tasted terrible as usual. It was a combination of trollex root for blood absorption, leaf of blood fig to improve problem-solving skills, and nightshade stems for skin clarity. Oliver knew that Bane always faked taking them. He considered doing the same, but sighed and swallowed it for real.

The pill was halfway down his throat when Bane slapped him violently on the back of the head. "Come on, lamb," Bane said sarcastically. "Don't want to be late for another great day at school!"

"Charles . . ." Phlox warned again, but Bane was already out of the room.

Oliver gagged for a moment, then got the herbs down and sullenly followed his brother.

CHAPTER 3

A Surprise at School

During the short days of winter, Oliver and Bane could safely use the surface streets to get around rather than the sewers and tunnels. They walked down Twilight Lane, then among the streets of human homes. Christmas lights twinkled on houses and in trees. A dreary mist fell on them as they walked. Though vampires didn't mind rain, the brothers wore long black coats at Phlox's insistence. Vampires could develop problems with mold if they weren't careful.

Oliver had a heavy backpack slung over his shoulders. He had to lean forward against the weight of the parchment texts inside. Bane had nothing with him. At the high school, where Bane and his classmates all had demons, classes were given using only spoken word. Bane used books now and then, for reference, but because demons had nearly timeless memories, and because vampires with demons would never bother with something as tedious as homework, Bane never had to bring a book to or from school. Of course, even if Bane had been required to, he likely wouldn't. School wasn't his first priority.

They passed under the looming girders of a high freeway bridge. Deep in the shadowy crux where the bridge met the rising slope of land, the humans had thoughtfully built a giant stone statue of a troll. From behind its massive head, two sets of eyes lit up in the murk, one yellow, one orange. Now an older boy spoke in a mocking girl's voice, "Oh, look at me, on my way to school like a good little rat-sucker should!"

Bane turned toward the eyes. "Shut up, Ty," he said, but smiled devilishly. Then he patted Oliver on the shoulder. "Have a good day at school, bro," he said, and hiked around behind the troll's head. His body disappeared in the dark and, a moment later, his eyes lit up as he joined the others. Oliver watched and heard hands slapping.

"Hey!" Bane shouted in Oliver's direction. "Run along, lamb!" Oliver turned toward school, his anxious feelings returning as he did so. It was hard to imagine that he would ever be like Bane and his friends: having a demon and acting like a grown-up vampire. At least, it wasn't expected of him now. *But soon, now that everyone thinks you're having the dreams,* he thought gloomily as he trudged along.

North Seattle Middle School was a looming brick building on a high crest of land, surrounded by large, bare-limbed trees and streets of small houses. It was old by human standards, built in the early 1900s. The paint around the windows was chipped. There were chunks of brick missing here and there. Human boys and girls still went there during the day, while the vampires secretly used it at night. Oliver wondered if the human kids thought it was a dump, but Oliver liked it. Phlox and Sebastian had made it clear that they would support Oliver if he wanted to apply to one of the private Underworld academies, but Oliver never had. It was bad enough feeling like he didn't fit in here. In the Underworld, things were even more intense. He couldn't imagine trying to act normal and not anxious around those Underworld kids.

He reached the back door, beside the blacktop basket-ball courts. It swung open, and there was Rodrigo, the night janitor. "Mr. Nocturne," he said in his soft voice, "Welcome, sir." Oliver nodded, wondering once again how the humans never noticed the points of Rodrigo's teeth, or that he wasn't breathing hard when he scrubbed the bathrooms — that he, in fact, wasn't breathing at all. Those who starred in human movies or worked for human news stations had to work a bit harder to keep their identities secret, but otherwise, vampires could work just about any night job in the city and be pretty sure that no human would notice what they really were.

Oliver headed up the wide stairs. The halls glowed in wild, shimmering neon. The painted murals and bulletin boards on the walls of the human school had been obscured by spectacular three-dimensional vampire graffiti art, called grotesqua. It was done in luminescent spray paint, a variety invisible during daylight, that Rodrigo activated each evening. There were demon faces, creatures from history and lore, and battle scenes that moved with neon figures fighting in silent motion. In some places, the glowing art resembled ancient hieroglyphics and runes. This was done by the older students, those who had begun to learn Skrit, the ancient pictorial language of the *vampyr*.

Oliver reached his classroom. The overhead lights were off, but a candle was lit on each desk, along with two on the empty lectern at the front. About half of his class of twenty had already arrived. A few boys were up on the walls, spray-painting glowing graffiti of their own with tiny silver cans. The girls were standing around the human children's fish tank, as their ringleader, Suzyn, carefully chose one of the tropical fish to eat. Oliver headed for his desk over by the windows.

As he passed under the back wall, he heard one of the boys above, Theo Moore, chanting ominously,

"Here comes the human, leaving school too late . . ."

Another boy, Brent, joined in, *"Go tell his mother, he's already been ate!"*

Theo lunged, landing on Oliver and slamming him to the floor.

"Ow, knock it off!" Oliver shouted, shoving Theo off him and jumping to his feet.

"Sor-ry." Theo frowned as he leaped back up onto the wall. "Guess the little lamb doesn't like to play the vampire games."

"Shut up," Oliver said, but too softly for the boys to hear. Theo had already turned his attention to the next student entering, and he and his friends resumed their chant.

Oliver reached the far row by the tall windows and slumped into his seat. "Hey, Seth," he said to the child beside him.

Seth was a short, round-faced boy with curly blond hair. He was laying a set of role-playing cards out in front of him. "Hey," he said absently, then laid a card, and frowned. "Osiris's army of light is totally kicking my butt."

"Too bad," Oliver said. He and Seth were considered friends, in so much as they sat next to each other and rarely hung out with Theo and his group. Seth's mother, Francyne, was on a few community councils with Phlox, and Oliver and Seth often ended up at the same adult events. Though they were good at hanging out and being bored together, Oliver felt like he and Seth were stuck with each other more than anything else, and Oliver never really knew what to say to him. Then again, he never knew what to say to most people.

Behind them, there was a flat smack as Theo landed on another student, and the others on the wall cackled. Oliver couldn't resist glancing back. One of his class's smallest students, Berthold Welch, was squirming his way free of Theo's grip, righting his glasses.

Oliver turned back to Seth. "Looking forward to Longest Night?" he asked, trying again to make conversation. Longest Night was the vampire celebration of the winter solstice.

"I guess," said Seth, raising his eyebrows. "Mom and Dad say I need to get my grades up if I want a bunny." He licked his teeth as he said it, and glanced over at Oliver. "Hey, you don't look so good."

"Oh — I'm just tired. I um . . ." Oliver scrambled to think of some acceptable excuse for why he looked so exhausted and landed on the familiar one before he could stop himself. "I started having the dreams, I think."

Seth looked impressed. "No way, really? Wow, I think you're the first. I haven't heard anyone else say that." He glanced around class. "You should tell Mr. VanWick, he'll probably give you less homework — have you tell your dreams to the class. Man, Oliver, you're lucky."

Yeah right, Oliver thought, cursing himself. Why had he started the lie again? "I . . . I'm not ready to tell anyone, yet," he said quickly. "Actually, they've been making me a little sick —"

Seth's eyes widened even further. "Wow, 'cause they're so intense? Maybe you're going to get your demon soon!"

It was official: Everything Oliver said just made things worse. "Oh, I don't know about that. My dad said it could still be a while. It might just be acclimation sickness or something." Acclimation sickness was almost like an allergy — when a child felt ill and out of sorts as their energies first joined with their demon. It was common and almost always passed before the demon actually arrived.

"Oh, yeah, could be," Seth said, but he was still impressed. "Man, if you get your demon first . . ." He gave a mischievous glance toward Theo and his gang on the back wall.

"Mmm." Oliver nodded. "Right now I just want to feel better. I've got my checkup on Friday though, so that should help."

Seth had started flipping over his cards again. "Your what?"

"You know," Oliver said. "Doctor's visit. Just the same old yearly checkup stuff."

Seth gave him a strange look. "You go to the doctor every year?"

"Yeah," Oliver replied. "Don't you?"

"I can't even remember the last time I went to a doctor," Seth said. "What would you need to go every year for?"

"You know, I mean, make sure you're healthy . . ." Oliver trailed off. His thoughts raced. *Because there's something wrong with you, obviously,* he thought.

"Healthy?" Seth said the word like it was from another language. "Your mom must be — ow!" Suddenly, something smacked Seth in the back of the head. "What the —"

There was a whoosh of air, and Oliver and Seth both turned to find Theo landing right behind their seats, flanked on either side by Brent and their friend Maggots. Maggots's real name was Rollie, but the nickname came from a case of the worms that he'd had since kindergarten and never fully gotten over, which often left him scratching at his head and feet.

"What, *Seth*?" Theo asked, smiling.

Seth reached to the floor and picked up the object

that had hit him: a rolled-up newspaper. He threw it back at Theo. "Knock it off!"

Theo was quick. He grabbed the paper in midflight, then smacked Seth across the head with it. "Careful!"

"Leave us alone, Theo," Oliver muttered.

"The cow-lover speaks!" Theo said, his eyes flashing at Oliver.

"Moo," Maggots added.

"What are you talking about?" Oliver asked. Theo was always looking for an angle to harass someone. His father, Grady, was a fairly notorious businessman in town, and kids at school knew that he was also fairly notorious when it came to punishing Theo. Which only made it harder to deal with Theo when he was being a jerk. "You're so stupid," said Oliver.

Now the newspaper was being slapped down on the desk in front of him.

"Check it out," Theo hissed in Oliver's ear. "You're front-page material."

In front of Oliver was the *Sea Lion Ledger,* the human kids' school newspaper. It had today's date on it. There were a bunch of articles laid out on the front page, but it only took Oliver a moment to see what Theo was talking about and, when he did, Oliver felt a sickening wave of worry. There, in the bottom left corner of the page, was a color photograph . . . of Oliver's house. The heading read:

In Search of the Vampires — Part 1
A Photo Essay by Emalie Watkins

Below that were the first few lines of the article:

> We all know the rumors, but what is the
> truth? Are there really vampires among us?
> In this exclusive story, we will search for
> evidence of the undead.
> *(Continued on page 7)*

"Come on, turn the page," Theo snapped, whipping the paper open.

Oliver watched, feeling like he might as well turn to dust. His thoughts were swirling. When he saw a four-photo spread of his house — the overturned dresser, the broken refrigerator, the peeling wallpaper, the putrid bathtub — Oliver actually felt a moment of relief until he read the short article running beside the pictures:

> This house at 16 Twilight Lane looks abandoned. But is it? Coming in next week's
> issue, my shocking photo of a real vampire
> who lives there.

"I —" Oliver began hoarsely.

Theo cut him off. "Dude, this girl has been in your house. She knows about the vampires. Is your family a bunch of human-lovers, or what?"

"No, we — I didn't know she knew we were vampires —" Oliver froze, realizing what he'd just said.

And so did Theo. "Wait, you *knew* this girl was in your house?"

"Well, I —"

"And you let her get away?! Ha! If that was me, I would've been like —" Theo bared his teeth and lashed his head forward. "Bang! Nosy human, dead human!" He shared a chuckle with Brent and Maggots. "But not you, Oliver. Figures. Couldn't do it, could you?"

"Um —" Oliver had no idea what to say. He looked frantically around the room, as if there was anywhere else to go. The entire class had turned toward the conversation. Seth was slouching as low as he could in his chair.

And Theo kept making it worse. "You know what I think," he said, "I think you *like* this human."

Snickers echoed around the room.

"No, I don't," Oliver muttered uselessly.

"Whatever," Theo went on. "If this girl has pictures of vampires, then *I* think she needs to get bit."

"We should find her," Brent added.

"She knows too much," Theo finished.

"Yum," Maggots agreed, scratching at his hair.

Oliver knew that none of them had ever bitten a human. Theo claimed to have tasted human blood, but Oliver thought it was all talk. Still . . .

"Hey, Oliver," Theo went on, rubbing Oliver's head. "We can save a bite for you since you like her so much —"

"Shut up!" Oliver shouted, and leaped to his feet. He grabbed the surprised Theo by the tie and slammed him backward. The two launched into the air, hitting the back wall five feet off the ground and cracking the chalkboard.

"No way!" Theo shouted hoarsely, Oliver's forearm against his neck. "Are you defending the human?"

Brent and Maggots were up on the wall in a moment. They wrenched Oliver free and hurled him across the classroom. Oliver lost his sense of up and down. He reached out to the forces without success and braced for a hard landing —

Only suddenly, he was stilled in midair, his body being controlled by someone else. Oliver opened his eyes to find himself suspended upside down just over the fish tank. Now his body flipped around, and he was thrust across the room toward his desk. As he flew, he heard the excited murmuring of students. He also saw Theo being pulled off the wall by an invisible force.

"Settle down, gentlemen," a low, gravelly voice hissed.

Oliver tumbled into his chair, then looked up to see Theo being dropped into his seat with a bone-jarring crunch.

Their teacher, Mr. VanWick, was sweeping into the room, coattails trailing behind him. "Students," he muttered, "that's enough horseplay." The boys and girls quickly scurried to their seats. Mr. VanWick reached the front of the room and tossed his leather briefcase onto the lectern. As he approached, a goblet, whose rim looked like it had never been washed, met his hand in the air. He took a sip, then looked out at the class and smiled. His flair for the dramatic dated back to having been an Underworld star of the stage in the 1700s. He had even appeared in early human silent films. Aside from the long hair growing from his ears, he kept his appearance youthful and perfect, despite his four hundred or more years. Only his eyes, deep in dark circles and red-rimmed, showed his true age.

Mr. VanWick continued, "Books to page one-eight-five." Everyone dutifully flipped open their parchment textbooks as Mr. VanWick cleared his throat and began to orate in his low steady voice.

Oliver managed to get his book open, his body still aching and his mind racing. He couldn't believe that article. Emalie had known about vampires. . . . She had that picture of him. If she printed it, Oliver's school and home life would officially be over. He would never, ever hear the end of it.

And Emalie's life would likely be over as well. A human writing articles about the vampires, no matter what little paper it was in, was also writing her own death sentence.

CHAPTER 4

A Missed Chance

Oliver sat quietly at dinner that morning, lost in thought. He absolutely could not let that photo appear in the paper. And he couldn't let Theo get to Emalie first. Oliver didn't think that Theo and his friends would kill her, but it would be bad enough if Theo got his hands on the photo she had taken. He could find many ways to torment Oliver with it. So Oliver had to get to Emalie before them, and definitely before any adult vampires noticed that article and started asking the Nocturnes why their house was featured in a human school paper. Because that would lead his parents all the way back to Oliver knowing about Emalie's visits.

He could imagine his parents' ashamed voices. *Why didn't you tell us? Or at least stop her from leaving that very first morning?* Yet the truth was that it hadn't even occurred to him to do so. And it would only be more embarrassing to explain that.

"How was school, dear?"

Oliver started, looking up like he'd been caught in a beam of sunlight, but Phlox was talking to Bane. The three of them were sitting in the low-lit dining room. Its walls were hung with deep velvet curtains, the magma-lights cooled to orange. A place was laid out for Sebastian, who wasn't yet home.

"Mmm." Bane's mouth was full of the chocolate soufflé they were dining on. "What a night," he added between chews. Oliver marveled at how easily Bane talked around the truth.

"Did you make any progress with physics class?" Phlox asked him.

Bane slugged back a gulp from his goblet. "Physics is stupid."

Phlox smiled tightly and looked down at her plate. Oliver knew that look. It was the calm before the storm. It made him nervous just to see it — it would be that look and more if his parents found out about this business with Emalie. "Physics is the key to learning to control the forces," Phlox said sweetly. She took a slow sip from her goblet.

"Whatever —" Bane began.

"It — is — not — what — ever," Phlox hissed. Her eyes began to glow turquoise. "You're barely keeping up with your studies as it is, Charles. You're almost eighteen. Do you want to be the only one in your class who still can't occupy?"

Occupying animals was a higher level vampire skill. It allowed vampires to merge spirits with certain dark animals, using them to travel, spy, or enter places unnoticed.

"Occupying is stupid, too," Bane snapped.

"Really?" Phlox replied, her eyes starting to smolder.

Something caught Oliver's eye from the corner of the room. There was a narrow shelf along the wall, with fire bonsai growing downward out of it, twisting their way in gnarled spirals toward an ornate iron bowl on the floor filled with swirling red magmalight. Beneath this display, a large brown rat was squeezing out from a crack in the stone wall. Its eyes were unnaturally black.

"Why do I need to travel in some lowly, living animal?" Bane was going on.

The rat crept up behind Bane's chair, then paused to stand on its hind legs. Wisps of black smoke began to rise from it. The feathers of smoke grew, twirling together, gaining weight and shape, and in moments, there was Sebastian. The rat drooped to the ground, looking exhausted, and slinked back into the rubble.

"It's a waste of time," Bane continued.

Sebastian stood just behind Bane, smoothing his suit jacket, pulling at his cuffs, even winking at Oliver. Then in a lightning stroke, he closed both hands around Bane's neck. Bane's eyes bugged. His goblet sailed out of his hand, clattering on the stone floor.

"Hmm," Sebastian said into Bane's ear. "I think occupying comes in rather handy, myself." He let go and moved to his chair, kissing Phlox before sitting down.

"How was work, dear?" asked Phlox, her eyes cooling back to hazel.

"The long nights never end," Sebastian said tiredly.

Bane rubbed at his neck, scowling. Oliver looked down at his plate, hoping Phlox might return to Bane.

"And how was your night, Oliver?" she asked.

"Oh — it was fine," Oliver replied as dully as he could.

"Remember, you have your checkup on Friday," said Sebastian as he scooped soufflé onto his plate.

"Oh, yeah." Oliver nodded.

"I don't get why the *lamb* has to go to these annual doctor's checkups," Bane muttered.

Oliver kept his head down, but listened carefully. He hadn't wanted to start any conversations, given the number of secrets he was currently dealing with, not even about Seth's strange doctor comments. Luckily, Bane had done it for him.

"Well, Charles," Phlox began. "There's been new research on what growing children need —"

"What he needs is some guts," Bane muttered sarcastically.

"Careful," Phlox countered.

Oliver dared to glance up — and found Sebastian looking at him. It was that odd look again, like Oliver was something to be studied. But then Sebastian smiled and turned away.

"Doctors, nutrition," Bane scoffed. "Why can't we live like Old World vampires? If we lived in Morosia, I'd be getting to raid human towns by now."

"That's enough," Sebastian said sternly. His eyes, brown like Oliver's, glowed fiercely, passing amber and nearing crimson. "There'll be no more talk of the Old World here. You can get your fill with your cousins next time we visit your grandparents, but until then, you will continue to *try* to become an enlightened being, and a part of the future, not the past." This was a topic that could anger him like no other. Even Bane sensed it and stopped.

Forks clinked against stone plates.

"I heard at Central Council today," Phlox finally said brightly, "that they're thinking of adopting a new policy on coagulants."

"Mmm," Sebastian chimed in. "The trade in blood concentrates has been out of hand for some time. Three dealers were convicted and incinerated for it last week alone."

And just like that, conversation moved on. Oliver only half-listened. His mind kept coming back to either the doctor or Emalie, and both had him worried.

❋

Oliver had an easy time waking up the next evening, mainly because once again, he'd barely slept. He was up long before his alarm, tossing and turning in the late afternoon. As four o'clock arrived and the winter sun set, Oliver got up and set yet another lie into motion.

Bane was still fast asleep. Phlox was bustling upstairs. Sebastian was gone early for work. Oliver hurried up to the kitchen.

"Oliver, you're up early." Concern filled Phlox's voice. "Trouble sleeping?"

"Nah," Oliver lied, leaning on the center island but not sitting down.

"Oh." Phlox seemed to relax. "The dreams then, huh?" She smiled. "Have you learned his name yet?"

"Who?"

"Your demon." Phlox sounded as excited as his gossipy classmates sometimes got. "Do you know where he's from?"

"I —"

"Oh, never mind. It's probably too soon." Phlox nodded. "I'm sure the settings and images are still confusing."

"Yeah," said Oliver, trying to sound disappointed.

"Well, in time —"

"I have that study group before school," Oliver blurted before Phlox said any more. "I told you." He kept his eyes off her, picking a spot on the low cabinets and staring at it.

"What study group?"

"For Multi-world Math." Oliver knew Phlox rarely forgot one of his activities. This was risky, for sure.

"And you told me when?" asked Phlox skeptically.

"Yesterday," Oliver said quickly. "I mean, I thought I did. I was supposed to . . . I don't *want* to go."

"Well . . . of course you should." Phlox nodded firmly. "You need to take every opportunity to keep your grades up. Um . . ." She opened the fridge and reached for a blood bag. "Okay then, I can whip up something quick for breakfast, I guess."

"Mom, I . . . I'm supposed to be there soon." Oliver couldn't stand the idea of sitting in the kitchen, eating beneath the weight of his lies.

"All right, here" — she rummaged into the cabinet and produced his herb pill — "take this, and this, while you walk." She reached into the fridge for a large jar that held tarantulas in suspension. The spiders were flash-fried to keep their fluids and venom in, then dipped in chocolate. Tarantula venom helped with quick healing, which was important, because recess play could get rough.

Oliver took the spider and hurried from the kitchen. Since it was still faintly light outside, he headed back downstairs and exited through a heavy wooden door by the crypt. He entered a short earthen tunnel that led to a second metal door. It slid open, and Oliver entered the main sewer line beneath Twilight Lane.

The sewer tunnels had all been built by humans. New World vampires believed that, whenever possible, there was no reason to expend the effort to build something, if there were these industrious humans around to do it for them. The same vampires at city hall who kept the houses on Twilight Lane safe from demolition also made sure that the major vampire tunnels were only worked on by night crews of city workers, and that these night crews were strictly undead.

Oliver walked along the edge of a wide tunnel composed of thick stone blocks. A shallow channel of rainwater ran down the center of the floor. Ornate lanterns glowed with mellow, golden magmalight. Recesses had been chiseled at regular intervals into the crux of the wall and floor. Each held a wrought iron candelabra, ablaze with thirteen tallow tea lights. The light from these cast twisted, larger-than-life shadows of the passersby up onto the walls and ceiling. Vampires loved this kind of simple distortion of reality into something artful.

This tunnel was a fairly major thoroughfare. And so, between the sconces, the dank walls were adorned with perfectly preserved oil paintings and tapestries: portraits of vampires that spanned millennia and majestic depictions of epic human battles. Oliver walked by a twenty-foot-long embroidered tapestry showing a legendary vampire, Klaus Virhaeten, whispering conspiratorially into the ear of the famous, and easily influenced, human general Alexander the Great. Alexander sat on a throne, in the shade of palm leaves, watching over a spectacular battle that flowed chaotically across the rest of the tapestry, displaying the grisly carnage of tens of thousands of men as no human artist would ever had dared to depict it. There was no artful "glory" or "heroics" in this depiction of war, just chaos and terror — humans at their most entertaining. The tapestry itself was almost as old as Alexander's empire, and a short-lived human historian would have nearly died if he'd ever found it. He would likely have whisked it away to a highly priced museum, but to the long-lived vampires, placing such a value on time seemed silly.

The sewer was fairly empty this early in the evening. A slow-walking old vampire woman was stopping at the intersection ahead of Oliver. From the opposite direction, a finely suited businessman huffed and flipped to the ceiling in order to pass her without having to put his brilliantly polished shoes in the water.

The woman stared at the blank concrete wall on the corner, then whispered, *"Anemoi."* The wall blurred and a map appeared, floating before her. It was a three-dimensional depiction of the sewer system and the streets above, drawn in tubular lines of light that sparked with bits of flame. The different areas and tunnel levels were drawn in different shades of the molten spectrum, from searing whites to warm magentas. The map resembled a square funnel, with the Underground Center dropping down out of the middle. The Underground was beneath downtown Seattle: It was the center of vampire life and spiraled deep into the earth. The woman pinched the corners of the map and twisted and turned it. It fluttered like fabric in front of her, sparking and hissing as she did so.

She then ran her finger through the image, pausing on a Skrit symbol, which flamed as she touched it. A soft, whispering voice announced, "Pioneer Tunnel Entrance: Access to charion lines B and C. One point two kilometer walk to the Underground Center. This is a force-persa accessible entrance." As Oliver passed the woman, she blew on the map, and it winked out of sight.

Oliver walked up another block, then stopped beneath a manhole cover high in the ceiling. He pressed a button on the wall, and the manhole slid open. Oliver leaped upward, shooting out of the sewer and landing in a narrow alley between two streets of quiet houses, only a block from school. It was almost dark now and rain fell from a featureless ash-gray sky. The colors in the alley were draining away with the darkness. Oliver hurried out to the busy street, awash in white headlights.

The last humans were still lingering outside of school: two kids shooting a basketball, a trio of girls sitting on the steps waiting for a ride home. As Oliver passed by, a silence fell over them. He headed quickly around back. Some classrooms were still lit, and large rectangles of warm light made plaid patterns on the wet blacktop. Oliver reached the back door and knocked softly. There was a moment of silence, then the door opened and Rodrigo looked out, speaking in his ever-tired voice, "You're a bit early, sir."

"Sorry, Rodrigo," Oliver said. "I . . . I need to do some extra work — can I come in?"

Rodrigo backed out of the way. "Just be careful," he warned. "There are still humans around."

"Got it," said Oliver. He headed downstairs, staying close to the wall, ready to spectralize. He'd seen signs for the humans' school newspaper in the basement art room and figured that was where Emalie and the other students met.

The only light in the hall came from the art room door, at the far end of the hall. Oliver stayed against the wall. As he neared the door, a tall, skinny girl popped out of a restroom, not two feet from him. She was three steps across the hall when she froze, glancing nervously over her shoulder. Oliver leaned back against the wall and spectralized, becoming only a shadow against the colorfully painted mural behind him. The girl gazed through him, but still darted quickly back into the art room.

Oliver moved to the doorway and scaled the wall. From the ceiling, he hung down and peered inside. The lights on the left side of the room were on. There were four students: two girls sitting at computers, one boy sitting at a high bench table — and, off in a dark corner, Emalie. She was holding her old camera under a bright lamp. She had the back open and was fiddling around with it. Her hair was in two braids. She wore her same lime green vest, an olive army jacket beneath it.

Oliver slipped through the door and up onto the classroom ceiling. He headed for the nearby corner and crouched, making himself as small as he could.

The two girls at the computers were giggling. They were chatting online. The boy was reading over some printed pages and editing.

"All right, everybody," said an older woman's voice. Their teacher's wide frame appeared in the doorway. "It's time to head home. Make sure you get your articles finished tonight."

The boy spun and immediately left. The two girls got up and started putting on jackets and hats. Emalie continued to study her camera.

"Ms. Davis said it's time to go, Emalie," one of the girls said in an unfriendly voice.

Emalie didn't answer.

The girl huffed, then rolled her eyes to her friend.

"She's so annoying," the other girl murmured, then turned back to Emalie. "Be careful you don't run into a *vampire* down here alone." The girls laughed as they left. For a moment, Oliver could hear them going on to each other in the hall, "What's her deal? Is she homeless again, or something?"

"Who knows? And what's with that ancient camera? It's like, afford a digital . . ." Their voices faded away.

Emalie muttered softly in a mocking tone, *"Afford a digital."* She shook her head.

Oliver stayed in the corner until their sounds and scents had faded. Then he crept a few feet closer, stopping as he reached a display of cut-out snowflakes hanging from the ceiling.

Emalie was still fiddling with her camera. "What's with you?" she muttered at it.

Oliver studied the snowflakes, thinking they were a bit simplistic-looking to be displayed in public. If he had set about making a paper snowflake, it would have been so much more ornate and detailed — then again, he'd had a few decades more practice with scissors and paper. *What are you doing?* he suddenly shouted at himself. Why was he thinking about snowflakes when he needed to talk to Emalie? He looked up at the clock. Five minutes had passed! Still, Oliver didn't move. How to start? Would he try to scare her, or reason with her? Would he tell her that he was a vampire? And how would she react? Maybe, since she was trying to prove that vampires existed, she'd be excited. Or maybe she'd be terrified and take off, and what would he do then?

"Oh, Emalie —" Ms. Davis had returned to lock the door. "Didn't know you were still here. You really need to get going."

"Sorry," muttered Emalie. She stuffed her camera into her beat-up canvas backpack and slid off the stool. As she walked out, Ms. Davis gave her a perplexed glance before reaching in and flicking off the lights.

Oliver dropped to the floor and kicked the nearest stool. A perfectly good opportunity and he'd blown it. *You're a lamb, just like Bane says!* he yelled at himself. Then he looked to the classroom clock: not even five thirty. He still had a while before school started.

Oliver headed back down the hall. He left out the back door and circled around the school. There was Emalie, walking up the street, alone. Oliver followed her, staying just over a streetlight-length behind her. She headed up the block, then turned and started across the ball fields. Oliver couldn't believe this girl was still alive with all the dangerous things she did. Crossing these fields alone in the dark? This was probably too dark a place to try introducing himself. He needed somewhere better lit. Oliver darted along behind her, moving from an old tree to the swings, to the basketball hoop, making sure there was some cover for him to blend into if she turned around, but she didn't.

Emalie passed through a border of trees, leaving the park, then stopped at the next street corner. She stood in a cone of light, mist falling on her, looking up and down the street, almost like she was deciding which way to go. Now she started fiddling in her bag. Oliver reached the edge of the fields. This corner would be a good spot, well enough lit that she might give him a chance. He started up the sidewalk —

A city bus pulled up. Emalie had drawn a bus pass from her pocket. The doors swung open and she stepped on board. Oliver was frozen. What now? Maybe he should just turn around, give up. Instead, as the bus pulled away, Oliver broke into a run. Twenty feet behind the bus, he leaped into the air, soaring upward. Pushing against the forces as hard as he knew how, he reached the top of the streetlights at the height of his jump, then arced downward, landing on top of the bus —

Only his jump wasn't perfect, and he immediately slid off the roof. Looking down, he saw the blur of pavement rushing up toward him. He grabbed at the side of the bus, tightening his grip on the forces, and just managed to hang on. He threw his body against the side, exhausted, and immediately spectralized as best he could, because many heads were peering out the windows just above him, wondering what all the racket had been.

The bus traveled a mile before Emalie got off. Oliver dropped off the side and sat down on the bus stop bench to rest, letting her go ahead of him. His muscles burned, and his mind ached from concentrating. Finally, he got up and followed Emalie's scent up a side street to a tiny, one-story house. Unlike its neighbors, Emalie's lawn didn't have any plastic, light-up Christmas figurines. There were no cheery lights strung on the trees or along the gutters, either. Oliver started up the walk, noting the overgrown yard on either side. Except for the light from the windows, this place almost resembled a vampire house.

He climbed carefully onto the porch, staying away from the rectangles of light. Inside, he saw a living room crowded with half-unpacked boxes. A tiny, artificial Christmas tree stood atop one stack. Its lights weren't plugged in. There was a crooked floor lamp by a table piled with dishes and papers. A man sat there, scratching his head and looking over a stack of bills. "Hey!" he shouted suddenly. There was no reply from the rest of the house. "I thought your *friend* said that the hot water was included in the rent!" Again, no one answered. The man drank from a beer bottle beside him, then shook his head. He had dark bags under his eyes. "Margie!" he shouted now. "Stop ignoring me!"

A light flicked on in the corner of Oliver's vision. Looking around the edge of the porch, he saw that it was coming from the basement, casting a small rectangle against the neighboring house. The light flicked off, replaced by a faint red glow. Oliver vaulted the railing and crouched to peer through the window.

Emalie stood in a small, square space, its walls made of boxes. She was leaning over a sink, and was lit only in red and shadow. Distantly, Oliver heard the man upstairs shout, "Come on, Margie!" to no reply. Emalie glanced up at the ceiling, frowning, then pulled earphones out of her vest pocket and slipped them on.

She bent back to the sink, where she picked up a pair of tongs and began shaking a piece of paper that was lying in a shallow tray of liquid. Oliver noticed a string along the wall with many photos hanging by clothespins. Oliver hadn't ever seen a darkroom before, but he understood basically what was happening. He watched through the window, with Emalie, as the paper she was shaking began to darken, and an image took shape. There was a wall, and something intricate and made of glass — a chandelier.

Now Oliver recognized the ceiling from the first floor of his house. She was developing the photo of him. He stood up, about to look for a way inside.

Suddenly, something sharp nudged him in the back, directly behind his heart.

"Don't move, demon," said a low voice from behind him.

CHAPTER 5

The Photograph

Oliver froze. He could already smell that the object was wood. And yet, he could also hear his enemy's short, quick breaths, and could smell that he was desperately scared. Oliver ran through his memory of scents and realized who it was.

In a lightning motion, Oliver leaped straight up into the air. He flipped around overhead, landing behind the figure. He lunged, grabbed the arm, and twisted it around the back.

"Ahh!"

The broken length of tree branch fell to the ground. Oliver pushed his attacker forward, pinning him against the foundation of the house.

"No!" Dean gasped, looking up at Oliver, wide-eyed. "I didn't mean it, I —"

Oliver bared his teeth. He wasn't actually sure what he was going to do next, but he definitely planned on terrifying Dean.

"Please don't kill me!"

"Stop it!" Oliver looked up to see Emalie racing around the side of the house. She had her own wooden weapon. It looked like the handle of a hammer, and it had been whittled to a sharp point. "Get away from him!"

Oliver let go and stood up. He thought about leaping up to the rooftop and taking off, but Emalie flicked a flashlight beam squarely on him. He winced and shielded his eyes.

Dean stayed slumped on the ground. He coughed weakly, pulling at the collar of his wool sweater.

"Dean!" Emalie cried. But she didn't go to him. She stayed a few steps away, flashlight and stake pointed at Oliver. She glanced back at Dean, her eyes furrowing angrily. "What were you thinking?"

Dean gathered his long arms and legs together and warily got to his feet, fixing his sweater and rubbing his short, black hair back into place. "I . . . I was just coming over for homework. I brought the Chinese." He gazed dejectedly at the grass, where a bag of Chinese food boxes lay spilled. "But then I saw him. I . . . I just thought I could —"

"Well, you can't," Emalie scolded. Her eyes turned to Oliver. "You're no match for a vampire."

Oliver tried to think of what to say. She knew what he was. It probably shouldn't have surprised him.

"You're the one from the house," Emalie continued, catching Oliver even more off guard.

"Yeah," was all he could manage to say.

She looked at him oddly, and what she said next surprised him. "Come inside."

"Emalie!" Dean blurted, but Emalie flashed him a stern look, turned and started around the house. "This is crazy," muttered Dean. He almost took a step, then stopped, instead motioning to Oliver. "You first."

Oliver shrugged and walked around the house, listening carefully to see if Dean tried to pick up his weapon. He didn't bother, instead gathering the Chinese food before catching up. "Emalie! Are you sure about this?" Dean called after her. Emalie didn't answer. "She's unhinged," Dean groaned quietly.

Oliver followed Emalie through a narrow door into the basement, weaving between piles of boxes to the cramped darkroom space, lit only in red. She returned to the sink as if Oliver wasn't there. Dean squeezed by, keeping a wary eye on Oliver, and put the food on a rusty washing machine along the wall.

"What's your name?" Emalie asked, bent over the sink.

"I'm Oliver."

"Oliver?" Dean mumbled. "That's not a very demon-like name —" Oliver turned toward him. He didn't even try to make a menacing face, but Dean immediately went pale. "Sorry," he said quickly. "It's a fine name."

"I'm not exactly a demon," Oliver started. "I —" But then he stopped. He didn't need to explain himself! He just needed to tell Emalie what he'd been meaning to all evening. "Look, Emalie, you're in danger."

Emalie didn't even seem surprised that he knew her name. "Why?" She started running water from the tap.

"The vampires know about your article."

"See?" Dean said accusingly. "I told you!"

This made Emalie stop. "How do they — how do *you* know about it?"

"Well . . ." Oliver explained as briefly as he could: how he attended the very same school at night, how his classmates had seen her story, and how they'd reacted. He left out the torment he'd taken for the mere possibility that he knew her. "If this gets out to the rest of town —"

"Whoa," said Dean, "What do you mean 'town'? H . . . how many vampires are there?"

"In this city," asked Oliver, "or this world?"

"W . . . world?" Dean sputtered.

Oliver decided not to overwhelm Dean with the latest census, which had this world's vampire population at almost a million. "There are about five thousand in Seattle."

"Five *thousand*?" Dean gasped. "That's — but, you'd need to kill people — to eat — there'd be hundreds of —"

"Not really," explained Oliver. "Vampires don't usually kill people. They just feed for a while, then give the human a potion that erases their memory. And there are salts that hide the bite wounds and make them heal almost overnight." Then Oliver glanced at Dean and thought to add, "You might have already been bitten and not even know it."

Dean rubbed nervously at his neck. "H . . . how many humans have you bitten?" he asked.

"I —" Oliver felt weird talking about all this. *Then why are you?* he wondered to himself. He wasn't sure, really. But was there any harm in it? "None," he said. "I mean, you don't, until you're older." He glanced worriedly toward Emalie, wondering if any of this was going to go too far and freak her out, but she was still working over the sink, almost like Oliver was no more important than whatever was packed in all these boxes.

"How much older?" Dean continued.

"It depends," Oliver said.

"Well, how old are you?"

Oliver wondered what to tell them. He looked thirteen in human years, and felt and acted thirteen as well, but the truth was, he was sixty-three years old. Vampires were thought to live forever, but what seemed like forever to a human was actually just very slow aging. A vampire aged about five times slower than a human. But wouldn't they think it was creepy if he told them he was almost five times older than they were? Then again, why should *he* care if they were freaked out? Still, Oliver decided on the easier number anyway. "Thirteen," he said, then returned to the reason he was here. "Listen, if you publish that photo of me, the vampires will — Well, just don't."

"I knew it," Dean said stiffly, "Knew it! We're dead!"

Emalie didn't answer. Oliver was starting to wonder what was wrong with her. "I'm serious," Oliver said.

"Is that what you came here to do?" she asked, still not turning around.

"Me? What?"

"To kill us?" Emalie stood up away from the sink now.

"No," Oliver stammered, "I . . . I just came to tell you to stop."

"Why?" Emalie asked, turning around finally. She looked at him seriously. Her eyes were startlingly clear. Whatever trace of fear Oliver thought he smelled wasn't showing on her face. And her gaze was making *him* feel weird.

"Um . . ." He wasn't sure how to answer her question. Telling her that he'd only come to save his own neck would make him sound selfish. Wait, why did he care how he sounded to these humans? This was ridiculous! But when he didn't answer, Emalie started talking again.

"Well, it doesn't matter," she said, holding up the photo from the sink, her face falling in frustration. "There is no picture. See?"

Oliver studied the photo in Emalie's hand. It showed his ceiling, with the cockeyed chandelier in sharp detail, but with only a big blurry spot beside it, where Oliver should have been.

"Just like all the others." She pointed past Oliver to the string of hanging photos. "Every time I try to print it, you just come out all blurry."

Oliver turned and looked at the photos. Among a number of shots of other places Oliver knew to be vampire hangouts around town were five copies of the photo that should have been of him. In every one, the area exactly where Oliver should have appeared was a wispy gray blur.

"I've tried printing it really dark," Emalie explained, "Overexposing it, changing the filter, the amounts of the chemicals . . . nothing works. There's something wrong with the negative." She tossed her tongs back into the sink with a splash. "So, I guess you'll get your wish."

"Not to mention we'll get to stay alive," Dean added, trying to sound hopeful.

Oliver stared at the photos. "It's weird," he said quietly.

"What?" Emalie asked.

"Vampires don't really use cameras," he said, thinking aloud. "It's usually drawings or paintings. I don't think I've ever had my picture taken before. I remember one time, my dad pulling me out of the way of a human camera."

"Why?" Dean asked.

"I don't know." Oliver had been too young to think to ask.

"So maybe cameras don't work with vampires. Like mirrors," Emalie offered.

"Maybe." But then Oliver thought about what he'd just said. He knew of people, like Mr. VanWick, or Ken Tempest, who'd been in movies or on television. *They* showed up on film. Unless video film was different — then again, he'd never looked for vampire photographs. He didn't know for sure that it didn't work. But why would his parents tell him cameras were dangerous? Was it that they were dangerous only for *him*?

"Maybe," Oliver found himself saying, "you need some ingredient you don't have."

"Like what?" Emalie asked. Her eyes narrowed with interest.

Oliver hesitated. He hadn't really thought through what he was saying, but Emalie's look made him feel like he should continue. "I don't know, there might be a special chemical — an enchanted solution or something."

"Enchanted?" Emalie looked even more curious. "What are you talking about?"

"Well," Oliver said. "I mean, vampires have access to science from the other worlds. I bet Dead Désirée would have something."

"Okay, wait," Dean said. He was squinting like his head was about to burst. "'Worlds,' with an 's.' Like more than one?"

"Well, yeah." Oliver tried to think of how to make sense of this for a human brain. "This" — he flicked his hand to indicate the world they were currently in — "is a middle world. There are higher and lower ones, too."

"Like how many?" asked Dean.

"Well, lots. I mean, there are infinite worlds. They're all different. This one, and the other middle worlds, are the only places where things are so — solid. In most of the others, demons don't take physical form. I mean, in some worlds, a vampire can't even be killed."

"So then why don't vampires go live there?" Emalie asked.

"Well," Oliver continued, "because we can't leave this world. We're sort of stuck here."

Emalie was staring at him. Then she shook her head. "Wow. Okay. So who's Dead Désirée?"

"She's an apothecary downtown, in the Underground."

"The Underground?" Dean asked.

"Yeah. It's like, the center of town, for the vampires."

"We should go," Emalie said.

"What? No," Oliver replied immediately. "No way — if a human ever got caught down there —" Not to mention the consequences for himself if he was ever caught bringing humans into the Underground.

"How about this weekend?" Emalie said seriously. Oliver couldn't tell if she was being sarcastic or had lost her mind.

"Emalie!" Dean protested.

"Oh, come on, cousin!" She wasn't exactly smiling, but she looked the happiest Oliver had ever seen her.

"Look, no," Oliver said firmly, shaking his head. "That's not happening." Still, amazingly, he found himself considering it. What was his problem? Emalie had him totally out of sorts.

"Come *on*," Emalie urged. "It's the only way you're going to see that photo."

"Why does anyone really need to see this photo?" Dean whined.

"No," Oliver said as seriously as he knew how. The fact that the photo couldn't be developed should have been the best news he could have heard. So why

would he want to *help* in getting it to work? Except —
he did.

"We could totally . . ." Emalie started.

Suddenly, a voice shouted from upstairs, "Margie!
Margie! You said we were going to eat soon!"

Emalie's face fell. "That's my dad," she said to Oliver.
"All right, forget it, then." All the air seemed to escape
out of her. She reached to the wall, where she flicked on
the regular light and turned off the red light. "Come
on, Dean," she said sullenly, brushing past him.

"Yup." Dean nodded, then glanced warily at Oliver.
"What about —"

"He can show himself out," Emalie said.

"But —"

Emalie looked right past Dean, to Oliver. "It was nice
to finally meet you, and thanks for the warning." She
half-smiled at him.

Oliver felt a rush of nerves. He tried to think of something to say.

"Désirée's," Emalie continued, gazing at him seriously. "Think about it. We could go this weekend."

"I —" Oliver began.

"Let's go!" Emalie's dad shouted, and Emalie disappeared into the boxes.

Dean awkwardly gathered the food, then gave Oliver
a last wary look. He sighed and turned to go, but
Oliver reached out and tapped his shoulder.

"Gah!" Dean gasped and dropped the bag once more.

"Sorry," Oliver said flatly.

Dean took a deep breath. "What?"

"Who's Margie?"

Dean looked at him quizzically, then his eyes flashed toward the ceiling. "Oh, that's Emalie's mom." Dean lowered his voice. "She's been gone for two years now."

"Gone where?"

"Nobody knows." Dean shrugged. He turned to go, then turned back. "So you're not going to kill us?"

"No."

Dean nodded like he was trying to believe it, but he still had a queasy look on his face as he left. When he was gone, Oliver turned back to the pictures of his house and his blurry form in them. What did it mean? Something . . . He felt like it meant something, for sure.

Before he left, he stepped over to the sink. Emalie had left a green hair elastic on the ledge by the faucet. With barely a thought, Oliver slipped it in his pocket. Then he headed back into the night, toward school.

CHAPTER 6

Now . . . and Then

That school night passed with Oliver barely noticing. He frustrated Seth by tuning out during their conversations, and he annoyed Theo, Brent, and Maggots by not even noticing when they harassed him. He incurred a brief, wrathful lecture from Mr. VanWick, because he was openly staring out the window during the night's history lesson. Gazing at the line of small houses across the street from the school, twinkling with Christmas lights, warmth radiating out of their windows, going dark one by one as the school night passed, he couldn't stop thinking about Emalie and Dean, and the photo.

"This is important, Mr. Nocturne." Mr. VanWick scowled, using the forces to slam Oliver's textbook against his desk for effect. The other boys snickered. "As a vampire, it is your duty to your society to be ready for the inevitable next time that human beings start killing one another. We must know the history that they keep themselves so ignorant of, so that we can act accordingly and enjoy the chaos."

"Sorry," Oliver muttered.

"Now then," Mr. VanWick continued, "today we continue our studies of the Aztec empire, a glorious period of human sacrifice unlike any other."

Normally, Oliver enjoyed history, but, no sooner had Mr. Van Wick continued orating than Oliver was lost in his own thoughts again.

At the end of the night, Oliver found himself hanging back as the rest of the kids quickly fled school. Once everyone was gone, he wandered the halls in the darkness. The neon demons were fading. The only light left was the slanting orange of streetlights through classroom doors.

He wasn't sure what he was looking for until he found Emalie in a photo outside a first-floor classroom. There she was, middle row to the right in her seventh-grade class, barely noticeable, wearing a sweatshirt, her hair in a bandanna, while all the other students were dressed up. Dean towered up from the back row.

He found Emalie and Dean again, in a chorus photo, farther down the hall. Emalie was singing in the picture, but her smile wasn't as bright as those of the girls around her. It looked forced. Oliver wondered if, like a vampire, music inherently made Emalie sad. Choral music was usually quite sad beneath its bright shiny surface, which made it a favorite of vampires.

Oliver ran over the conversation in Emalie's basement again, thinking about her request to go to the Underground, thinking about how he did want to see that photo. Distracted as he was, Oliver found himself eyeing a framed photo on the other side of the door. He now noticed that Emalie and Dean's chorus photo had the word *Now* above it, and above this other photo were the words *and Then*.

The black-and-white picture showed a school chorus from long ago. The students were dressed much more formally: the boys with their hair slicked back, the girls with bows. And there, in the middle row of the photo, was a vampire. She would have been hard for a human to spot, but it was obvious to Oliver, despite the cheery bows in her hair and the smile on her face. A vampire in a human school chorus? Oliver remembered something from history class, about how vampires early in the last century had tried to live among the humans. They had called themselves Conformists. They had gone to great lengths, even using special creams to withstand sunlight, but in the end, it hadn't worked out. The Conformists were considered a shameful chapter in vampire history.

But wait — Oliver was looking at a vampire *in* a photograph. If this girl could appear clearly in a photo, then why hadn't he? Had the Conformists done something special? Or was the truth what Oliver was starting to suspect, that vampires *could* appear in photos, and it was only Oliver who couldn't?

Oliver stared blankly at the photo, his head lost in confusing thoughts. What was wrong with him that he couldn't be photographed? After a while, he swam out of his head and realized that his gaze had drifted away from the vampire girl. Now he was staring at the face of the young music teacher standing to the side of the class. She looked happy, her hair up in the curls of the time, a wide smile on her face —

Suddenly, there was a flash in Oliver's mind — a vision that seemed clearer and stronger than any dream. It was this woman's face, smiling, looking down toward him tenderly. Behind her there were strange, tiny lights, and formations, maybe buildings, it was hard to tell, because he was overwhelmed by her bright human eyes.

Oliver shook his head, and the image blinked out, leaving his vision bleached in white spots, like he'd been staring at a streetlight for too long. He looked down and found himself trembling — but why? Who was that woman? It had almost seemed like a memory.

Maybe he'd seen her when he was little. It was always amazing how your brain could remember the strangest little details from so long ago. Yet, why would his brain remember this face out of the thousands he'd seen? And for that matter, why did Oliver feel his anxiety creeping over him now? His insides were getting tight. He wanted to study the picture more carefully —

Just then, two hands grabbed him by the shoulders and hurled him down the hall.

"Wha —" Oliver sailed through the air, slamming onto the tile floor and sliding into a trio of trash cans.

"I'm waiting out there for *ten* minutes." Oliver looked up to see Bane marching toward him, his green eyes blazing in bright lime.

Oh, no, Oliver thought. Bane had been waiting for him to walk home from school. Now he reached Oliver and yanked him to his feet by his backpack.

"Ow!" Oliver shouted.

"Come on, little lamb," Bane sneered, dragging him stumbling down the steps toward the back door.

"That hurts!" Oliver protested, thinking, too late, *No! Don't say anything!*

But he had, and now Bane whirled toward him. "That hurts? *That?*" His nostrils flared and his eyes sparked. "Well, try this!" He grabbed Oliver's shoulder and hurled him through the air. Oliver hit the back door, slamming it open, and tumbled out onto the now-deserted playground.

He slowly got to his feet, gathering his bag and

rubbing his sore head. But then Bane was grabbing him again. "Oh, come on, already," Bane muttered, and pushed Oliver toward the side of the school.

"Knock it off." Oliver muttered, getting his feet under him and stalking off toward the street.

"Oooh," Bane chided. "Watch out."

Oliver kept walking, and Bane fell into step beside him. Oliver glared up at him, but saw that the light had faded from Bane's eyes. Now, he actually threw an arm around Oliver's shoulders. "You gotta toughen up, bro," he said reasonably. Then he continued, "Something's going on with you. Older brother can tell."

Oliver's anger immediately cooled to freezing worry. "Um —"

"Not sleeping at night," Bane went on. "Lying to get to school early . . ."

They left the schoolyard and proceeded through the silent streets of sleeping houses. Oliver was shocked by Bane's change of attitude. Why was he suddenly acting like he cared? "You're a vampire, for Hade's sake," Bane went on, and even patted Oliver's shoulder. "When I saw you in there just now, you looked like you were about to cry or something."

Oliver bit his lip, afraid to say anything. He did not trust this strangely concerned version of Bane, though at least he didn't seem to know about Emalie or the newspaper. Oliver tried to think of anything he could say to change the subject. "I . . . I'm just stressed about my homework."

Bane sighed. "Homework sucks," he agreed. "It's a tough world, Ollie," he said in a tone that was so brotherly that Oliver almost laughed at how strange it sounded. "I had a lot of hard years, waiting for my demon to finally show up." A note of bitterness had entered his voice. "But then you get to make up for it." He patted Oliver's shoulder again. "You sure there's nothing else going on?"

"Not really," Oliver lied. His head was throbbing less, but the ache was a reminder of what Bane might do if he knew about Oliver's interaction with the humans. "Just, school sucks, that's all."

Bane didn't reply for a moment. Oliver glanced up at him, and found his brother eyeing him oddly. *He knows,* Oliver thought, his nerves humming. *He doesn't know what, but he knows there's something.*

Finally, Bane shrugged. "Totally," he agreed. "But listen, you ever want to talk about anything, you let me know," Bane finished. "It's always better to talk about things before they get out of control, you know?"

Again, Oliver felt that weight to Bane's words. "Yeah, okay," he said, hoping that would be the end of the conversation. And it was. But Oliver didn't trust Bane, brother or not, to leave it at that. He'd have to be very careful.

✸

Dinner was even less enjoyable than the previous night had been. Oliver was beginning to wonder how long he could keep living these lies. And beneath them, he was as confused as ever by the photo mystery.

"And how was your math help this morning?" Phlox asked.

"Fine," Oliver said quickly, gulping wolf's blood from his goblet.

"You're making progress?" Sebastian asked.

"Mmm," Oliver replied, now shoving a heaping spoon of crème brûlée into his mouth.

"Good," Sebastian said. Oliver looked up to find him gazing curiously across the table. Dad looked down, taking a sip from his goblet. "Ollie, don't forget, I'm picking you up tomorrow for your doctor's appointment. I'll meet you at school."

"Okay."

"Yeah," Bane piped up, "so don't get all weird staring at the human pictures and losing track of time like you did today." He flashed a hint of a grin, then continued eating.

Oliver wanted to kill him.

"What are you talking about, Charles?" Phlox asked.

"Nothing," Oliver interrupted quickly. "I was just looking at old photographs."

"Of *cows*," Bane added, eyes on his food, as if he were saying the most unimportant thing.

"Human photographs?" Phlox shared a sideways glance with Sebastian. "What would be interesting about those, dear?"

Oliver tried to think of something to say, but all he could think of was the blurry photo of himself, and how his parents had told him to avoid cameras. He knew he should just make up some excuse, but then he surprised himself by saying: "I don't know, I just — I saw a vampire girl in one of the old photos."

"Ahh," Sebastian said, sighing like he was relieved, yet not making eye contact with Oliver. "Well, yes, for a while, some vampires tried to blend in with humans. They were called Conformists, but they —"

"But I thought," Oliver interrupted, "a vampire couldn't get their picture taken?"

Phlox and Sebastian traded another lightning-fast glance. "Well," Sebastian said, picking up his napkin and dabbing at his mouth, "back then, it was different, it —"

"Didn't you tell me it was dangerous?" Oliver asked, trying to sound as innocent as he could.

"You lamb," Bane chuckled. "How could a camera be dangerous?"

Phlox sipped from her goblet. Sebastian looked at Bane, but not with anger, almost with confusion. Both his parents seemed to be looking anywhere except at Oliver. He watched them, watched their faces twitch, and now he felt like he knew for certain. *There is something going on here,* he thought. *All this means something.*

"Well, Oliver," Phlox began. "Photographs just aren't done. They're unseemly and a proper vampire would much prefer a painting or —"

Oliver took a chance and interrupted again. "But, that's not the same as dangerous —"

"They're dangerous for you, son," Sebastian said quickly. "Now, it's nothing you should *worry* about, but, it's the flashes, too. And you know how you get anxious —"

Phlox jumped in. "You're very sensitive to certain kinds of light spectra."

"I am?" asked Oliver. This was news to him.

"Yes," Phlox added. "Many vampires are. That's part of why cameras just aren't used in our world."

Oliver nodded. "Oh," he said.

A silence fell over the table.

Oliver kept quiet through the rest of dinner. He'd never felt anything like this before, the suspicion that his parents were keeping things from him. That they might even be lying to him. Sensitive to flashes? Oliver had just *had* his picture taken with a flash — and he'd been fine. As he thought about what his parents had said, Oliver found that his same old worried thought, *There's something wrong with me,* now had a different ending: *And maybe my parents know what it is.*

Oliver slept worse that day than ever before. In fact, he wasn't sure that he'd slept at all. The one thought that cheered him up was hoping he'd hear a footstep upstairs — that Emalie and Dean might show up again, but they didn't.

CHAPTER 7

The Doctor and the Moonlight

Oliver waited outside after school the next night. He sat on the front steps as the rest of the students caroused about. Finally, as the last stragglers were wandering home, he heard the rustling of a crow's wings. A shadow of a bird landed in a pool of orange streetlight out on the sidewalk. Swirls of black mist rose from it, and moments later the bird flew off. Sebastian hurried up the walk, his boots clicking in the stillness, the collar of his long black coat upturned against a cold, clear night.

"Sorry I'm late," Sebastian groaned, checking his watch as they hurried down the street. "Things are particularly busy at work." He didn't sound happy about it.

They reached a wide intersection, silent at three A.M. save for the hum of the streetlights and the clicking of the traffic signal from red to green. Sebastian checked his watch. "We'll take a cab," he said. "I put a call in to Miles. He should be along soon."

A moment of silence passed. A hunched man in a hooded jacket hobbled by, pushing a shopping cart. Oliver wrinkled his nose. It was a human, but his scent was so neglected, so shrouded in death, that he might easily have been mistaken for a zombie. In vampire terms, he was *spoiled* and a sad waste. Phlox had a friend, Chloe, who volunteered in human soup kitchens, trying to rehabilitate cases like this. She would add special ingredients to the free meals in order to help detoxify the poisoned blood. It was rare, though, for a human to come back from a condition like this homeless man was in. Oliver listened now as the man mumbled to himself, following well-worn loops of thought over and over. He could feel the despair, the whole rooms of a once bright mind that had shut down, and he wondered how humans could let one of their own get to that point.

"This will be good," Sebastian said, clapping Oliver on the back.

Oliver didn't reply.

"Dr. Vincent always helps when you're having" — Sebastian paused like he was looking for a word — "issues."

Oliver felt like asking Sebastian what issues he was

talking about. After all, Dad thought Oliver was having the demon dreams, didn't he? That should have been a good thing. So, then he must have been referring to how Oliver had been caught looking at human pictures. That didn't seem like it was enough to be an *issue,* unless Dad knew more about what had been going on with Oliver lately than he was admitting. Oliver was starting to wonder if Dad had believed his lie about the demon dreams at all.

But Oliver was looking forward to this doctor's trip. These visits had helped with his anxiety and trouble sleeping in the past. *Except those other times, you didn't know that you're the only kid who needs to go to the doctor every year.* Oliver promised himself that he would try to pay more attention to what Dr. Vincent said this time, to see if he could gather what these visits were really all about.

"It's always hard for you around this time of year," Sebastian continued. "Just remember, Ollie, you're a very special boy." He eyed the passing vagrant. "A special boy among a special breed. Vampires are lucky, compared to the humans. We get to experience and perceive things they could never fully grasp. Their lives are so short. They approach everything either with desperate passion or desperate fear. Their world can seem vital and interesting, but only because they are so ignorant."

"Okay," Oliver said. He didn't understand what his dad was getting at, except the words were making him feel defensive about Emalie and Dean. Vampires always talked about humans like they were lower beings, but Oliver hadn't felt that way about Emalie, though maybe slightly about Dean. And it almost sounded as if Sebastian was trying to talk Oliver out of any interest in humans. *Because he knows,* Oliver thought worriedly. Or, if he didn't know, he at least suspected.

A cab screeched to a halt beside them. Sebastian leaned down and peered in the window, then smiled. "Hello, Miles." He nodded, opening the door. Oliver slid into the backseat beside him.

"Good evening, Nocturnes," Miles Frisht said with a feigned air of manners. "Where can Miles whisk you off to on this lovely eve?" He was a gangly vampire, wearing a beat-up cowboy hat cockeyed on his head and flashing his one remaining eye at them.

"Dr. Vincent, at the Gasworks," said Sebastian.

"Aye." Miles nodded, and sped off, cueing the radio to life as he did so.

In contrast to Miles's ragged appearance and the chaotic way that he careened around town, the music that filled his cab was a deeply sad string quartet. Oliver glanced forward to see that they were listening to KBYT, a vampire pirate station that played from midnight until dawn. Other than Bane and those his age, who preferred the latest meta-world dub, broadcast subversively on the human station KEXP, vampires mostly listened to deeply complex classical music. Oliver recognized what was currently playing: the familiar haunting melodies from one of the late movements of the *Melancholia,* the master-work of vampire music. Its early movements were cen-turies old, and it was still being added to. The full piece was rarely performed and, when it was, it was a fan-tastic event, as it took over two months to play every movement. Hearing it now, Oliver felt himself relax just a bit.

A few hectic turns later, they were pulling up to the Gasworks. "Thanks, Miles," said Sebastian, handing him three square silver coins with holes in the center, called *myna*, a currency that vampires had used since ancient Greece, in situations where other forms of pay-ment, like a fresh young animal, or bone credits, weren't practical.

They started across a long grass park along the edge of a wide lake, just north of downtown. In the center of the park was a labyrinth of black metal towers: an old gas refinery long shut down. It was surrounded by a high chain-link fence that kept the contaminated site safe from humans. The hulking cylinders stood in dark silhouette against the blinking city buildings and the glowing Space Needle, across the water.

A raw wind peppered Oliver and Sebastian with spray from the lake. They leaped nimbly over the fence, and Oliver followed his dad as they lost themselves in the maze of black metal towers spun together with catwalks above. Their shoes clattered on a bed of gravel and rust flakes.

Sebastian stopped at a black tower no different than the others, except that three stories up, near the top of the tower, there was a single, glowing silver Skrit symbol: an upside-down eye inside a square. He knocked on the metal wall, creating a hollow thud. For a moment, there was no response, then the squealing echo of deadbolts being turned. A curved rectangular door pulled inward, and warm light spilled out. Oliver followed Sebastian in.

In stark contrast to the decrepit exterior, inside Oliver found himself in the nicely appointed waiting room. It was small, lit with low lamps, and lined with chairs, three of which were filled: two with older women and one with an extremely ancient man who had long since lost his skin to time. His teeth were still brilliant white, and he wore a tweed suit with a bow tie. Oliver had rarely seen a man so old and guessed he might be well more than six hundred.

Sebastian moved to the receptionist's desk, where a striking young woman sat at a computer. "Nocturne to see Dr. Vincent," he said. Oliver sat down, and watched as his dad popped open his briefcase and removed a plain-looking legal folder, which he handed to the receptionist. Oliver recognized his medical records. He looked down at the stack of magazines on the table beside him: *Seattle Tombs and Flats*, *Bloodlust*, *Us Weekly* . . .

"Hell's speed to you, my boy," a razor-thin voice hissed from beside him. Oliver turned to find the ancient man leaning toward him, his leathery face only inches from his. The whites of his eyes had long since turned to black, and his pupils had dulled to a luminous gray that indicated almost total blindness. His wrinkled nose was doubly active, sniffing the air between them. Oliver could smell the time on him.

"Hi," Oliver said, trying to be polite.

"I hope he comes to you soon," the man hissed, the effort of speaking making his body shake.

Oliver nodded respectfully, not knowing what the old-timer was talking about.

"The wind wants to take me as dust," the man went on, "But I tell it, *No, Illisius is coming, and I don't mean to rot to dust before we're finally freed from this prison!* That's what I tell that cursed wind." The man's teeth clicked eagerly.

"That's great," Oliver said, and turned back to the magazines —

But the man grabbed Oliver's shirt collar with his bone hands and spun him around. "Don't take your destiny lightly, Oliver. You are the one who can open the Gate." He pulled Oliver even closer, with ten times the strength Oliver would have thought possible. His skinless face stretched into a grin. "You are he who will journey to N —"

A hand firmly pushed the old-timer away. "Excuse me, sir," said Sebastian sternly. "Have to get my boy in for his checkup. Come along, Oliver." Dad was smiling, yet he quickly pulled Oliver up out of his chair.

The man was scowling at the interruption, but then broke into a wide smile. "Yes, yes," he cooed. "Off to the doctor for the vessel! Careful with my merchandise! I'm not to dust before the ascension!"

Sebastian moved Oliver quickly across the room. "Never mind him," Sebastian said, before Oliver could even form a question as to what the old man was talking about.

The smiling receptionist held open a dark wooden door. She led them down a short hallway to an elevator. Brass doors slid open, revealing a cylindrical copper elevator car.

"The doctor will see you in exam room three," the receptionist said, her smile unbreakable.

The doors slid closed. Three was the top floor. The elevator began to rise.

"Old ones are like that," Sebastian started saying. "He's almost at the end. It could be another century, or maybe only decades. It's a confusing time for them. What was he saying to you, anyway?"

Oliver shrugged. "I couldn't really understand him," he said, yet another lie coming so easily. Oliver supposed the old one was off his rocker but, still, what was that all about? It had seemed like he'd known something about Oliver.

The elevator slowed, and the doors slid open, revealing a wide, circular room. Floodlights stood on metal stands, beaming white light into the center of the room. The effect made the dark iron walls seem almost invisible. In the center of the room was a standing contraption. It was folded open like a clamshell, each side made of silver mesh shaped like a body. Oliver stiffened when he saw it. Even though he'd been in the force resonance imager before, the sight of it always made him squeamish.

"Ahh, Ollie, welcome," a friendly voice echoed from the darkness, and Dr. Vincent emerged from the shadows behind the lights. He was a young doctor, maybe 250, with broad shoulders, a chiseled face, and slicked blond hair. Oliver had heard his parents say on more than one occasion that they were lucky to have such a young, bright physician around. Dr. Vincent had worked for years in research in the asylum colony of lower

Morosia, a highly respected facility, if controversial for its methods.

Dr. Vincent buttoned his white coat and stuck out his hand as Sebastian and Oliver reached the center of the room, their footfalls echoing loudly on the metal floor. Oliver put out his hand, and the doctor shook it vigorously.

"Hi," Oliver said.

"Good to see you, sir," Dr. Vincent said to him, smiling, then turning to Sebastian. "Seb, nice to see you, too," he said warmly.

Sebastian handed him the manila folder. "Just the usual checkup today, Doctor?"

"Annual physical, same as always," Dr. Vincent said cheerily. "So? Oliver, ready?"

Oliver stepped up to the open, body-shaped FRI shell and turned around, backing into half. As his back met the cold metal, he shivered, feeling a ripple of worry, but he reminded himself that he was hopeful: *Maybe this is all you need,* Oliver thought, wondering if that could be possible.

"Here we go," Dr. Vincent said. He strapped Oliver's arms in place at his sides, and then his ankles. Now he stepped back and shut the front half of the shell closed. As soon as the latch clicked, there was a sound like ruffling fabric, and the entire mesh shell shrunk and tightened to fit exactly around Oliver. The silver threads pressed cool against his face. No movement was possible except for his eyes, and his view was blurred by the mesh. Oliver vaguely saw Sebastian taking a step back. Oddly, he didn't look like he enjoyed watching this.

Dr. Vincent turned to a console beside the imager. Its brass surface was inlaid with controls and gauges. He pulled a lever and a deep humming overwhelmed Oliver's senses. Oliver felt himself beginning to rise. The imager moved steadily upward, stopping when his feet were equal with the doctor's shoulders.

"All right, Oliver," Dr. Vincent said, dialing in settings on the console. "This will be the standard checkup. You'll feel some electric conduction as the imager identifies your force readings. As they start to appear in spectrum around you, you might get a little light-headed."

Oliver was sure he would. The process always put him to sleep.

The machine began to vibrate. Oliver could feel the electric current running through his body, charging particles and heating up the forces. The doctor fiddled with more knobs. Sparks began to softly crackle along the threads encasing Oliver. There were blues, greens, oranges, and then colors across the spectrum. Light began to jump out from the imager, making arcs like solar flares that spiraled around him.

Oliver could feel heat and his body vibrating lightly. The colors increased in brilliance. Now Dr. Vincent backed away and began to appraise the show of spiraling colors. A computer screen lit up in the shadows behind him and began recording data.

Oliver had a basic idea of what was happening. Vampires were powered by forces. Some of those were life forces, supplied by blood, yet many were crossover forces, from other worlds. Those things that humans called mystical power, or enchantment, were really just the brief appearances, in this world, of forces from somewhere else. Because vampires were undead, they were just disconnected enough from the reality around them that they could feel those forces. Oliver only understood those basics. Vampire scientists and scholars spent centuries trying to understand the physics of the parallel worlds.

The mesh cage was a special receptor for forces and showed their presence and intensity in shades of the color spectrum. Every vampire had a unique signature of forces. Dr. Vincent was reading Oliver's now.

And yes, the light show, and humming, and warmth of the electricity was making Oliver sleepy. His eyes began to flutter. The buzzing and light was all around him. It was peaceful. Oliver's eyes fluttered closed and he fell into a deep sleep.

Except the sleep didn't last like it usually did.

Oliver usually woke up when the machine had shut off, but this time he came to early, overwhelmed by the familiar anxious feeling that always kept sleep away. His eyes snapped open.

He found himself lying flat on his back. He was still in the FRI cage, but it had rotated, so that he was looking straight up at the ceiling. And the ceiling had opened. Brilliant, pale white light was flooding down. Oliver squinted and saw the full moon directly overhead and a ring of mirrors around the rim of the open rooftop. They were gathering the moonlight, focusing it down through the roof — and onto him.

Straining to look toward his feet, Oliver could see that his whole body was surrounded by a bone-white glow. No, it *was* his body that was glowing, like he was absorbing the moonlight. Just then, a humming that he hadn't noticed revved to a higher pitch. The mirrors brightened. The intensity of the light increased, and Oliver's glow increased as well. He felt a cool, tingly surge through his body.

What was going on? He never remembered this happening during a checkup before. But then again, the FRI had usually knocked him out. Had this *always* happened and he just never knew it? Then Oliver heard a voice from beside him.

"Almost finished," Dr. Vincent said softly. "I'm giving him a longer dose than usual. The increased vessel strength should also make his anxieties calm down." Oliver peered out of the corner of his eye. Dr. Vincent and Sebastian were standing in the shadows by the computer console. Dr. Vincent was writing in the manila folder. "Now, you say," he continued, "that there's been some insomnia, and you think, some form of human sympathizing syndrome."

"I . . . I can't be sure," Sebastian murmured, sounding worried, "I mean, he won't admit anything's wrong, but . . . Listen, you don't think we did — we've done — something *wrong* to him, do you?"

"No," Dr. Vincent said with a professional's certainty. "Everything's been done according to the oracles, and according to the best scientific theory. Unless there's some leftover issue on account of his origin."

"How could there be?" Sebastian asked in a hush.

"I don't think there is," Dr. Vincent assured him.

But Sebastian continued, "I mean, we did everything right, didn't we? And even so, there's no way he should be able to remember any of that. He was a baby."

"Of course not." Dr. Vincent paused. "Though there was that odd reading in his initial workup. But that was so many years ago now, and it's never shown up again."

Sebastian's tone grew dark. "You told us he would be fine."

"Look, Seb, he *is* fine. Everybody's wired differently. Kid's probably just scared about growing up. Who isn't?" Dr. Vincent went on, "The bottom line is, all my readings show that these treatments are working. A little anxiety is a small price to pay. Besides it shouldn't surprise you. Part of your reason for choosing Oliver over all the other profiles was his emotional capacity, and I'm confident these treatments will keep the anxiety in check."

"But what if they don't?"

There was a pause, then Dr. Vincent said, "Well, there's always been a chance he could go insane. But insanity has certain advantages, and that's treatable, too."

"Not if it destroys him," Sebastian noted.

"True, but even if it does . . . we can always try again."

Sebastian only sighed.

Oliver struggled to make sense of what he was hearing. What treatments? Weren't they just checkups? Why would they make him go insane? And what had happened to him when he was a baby?

Now he felt another surge of the focused moonlight energy. It felt like his body was humming from head to toe.

"All right, that's it," Dr. Vincent said, and with the flick of a switch the mirrors went dark. Oliver's moon glow faded, and large gears started to grind. The ceiling slid closed. The cage began to rotate Oliver back to a standing position.

Oliver closed his eyes most of the way, yet watched, squinting, as Dr. Vincent scribbled final notes in the folder, and then handed it back to Sebastian, who already had his briefcase open.

"Tell your bosses not to worry," Dr. Vincent added. "Though I'm hoping you haven't mentioned these little anxiety bouts to them."

"No, I haven't," Sebastian muttered.

"I think that's best. The Half-Light is too jittery as it is, in my opinion. Things are fine."

"Mmm," Sebastian replied absently as he closed his briefcase and spun the locks.

The cage reached an upright position. Dr. Vincent approached, holding a clear syringe. The fluid inside was a swirling silver. Oliver shut his eyes fully and tried to look fast asleep, forcing himself not to wince as the needle stuck into his arm. He felt a surge of awakening spread through him. He waited another moment, then opened his eyes to find Sebastian and the doctor appraising him with relaxed smiles.

Dr. Vincent unstrapped Oliver and helped him down. "Welcome back, kiddo."

As Oliver steadied his wobbly legs, Sebastian clapped him on the back. "You never can make it through the imager without a nap, can you?"

"Guess not," Oliver said with a grin.

But inside he wasn't smiling. As they left Dr. Vincent's office, Oliver watched his dad treat him normally, the doctor treat him normally, the receptionist . . . And yet, he wasn't normal, was he? Oliver didn't understand most of what he'd heard, but he understood enough to know that whatever was wrong with him was much more than just some sleepless nights. It was something that everyone seemed to know about, except him.

Unlike in past years, Oliver felt no better after the visit. The rest of that night and through the sleepless day, Oliver's head spun. Who was in on it, whatever *it* was? His parents, Dr. Vincent, and it sounded like the Half-Light Consortium, too. What about Mr. VanWick? What about the other kids at school? Did their parents know? Bane?

And how could Oliver find out what they knew? Nobody would tell him if he asked, would they? Besides, that would just show them that Oliver knew something was going on. That didn't seem like a good idea. Were Emalie and Dean really his only choice? But how could *they* help him figure out what was going on? Well, maybe there was a way, but it wasn't going to be easy.

CHAPTER 8

Into the Underground

That Saturday, a long rain gave way to a deep foggy night, which hid each hill of the city from the other. The Space Needle was devoured to its waist. Gaps between houses became voids of the unknown. The cones of misty light beneath streetlights became islands of safety. In the downtown shopping center, the Christmas lights that covered every store entrance created a world of cheeriness that felt like a haven separated from the rest of the raw night. Here, revelers gathered to ride a merry-go-round, get fun family pictures, and go to a choral concert, the kind of somber music that few humans listened to unless it was the holidays.

The All-State choir performed beside a giant Christmas tree, which was almost as bright and cheery as the trendy coffee shop beside it. A crowd stood huddled together against the mist, listening as the pure young voices sang. They were finishing Handel's *Messiah*, singing stirring chords sad enough to move even the silent hearts of the stone gargoyles that watched from their perches two stories up — with Oliver crouched on a thin ledge between two of the winged creatures.

The conductor snapped his arms and the chorus went silent, their last note echoing upward until it was swallowed by the fog. There was a deathly moment of quiet as the depth of the song lingered, then the humans began to clap. Now the choir burst into "Jingle Bells." Oliver watched as, while more humans joined the crowd to revel in the cheery music, a few others gathered their kids and turned to leave — vampire families.

Yet two humans also turned and departed. They'd been standing with a set of adults and two other gangly children. They pushed their way to the edge of the crowd, looked warily about, then headed across the plaza, toward the edge of the cheery light.

Oliver slipped off the ledge and crawled down the wall headfirst. When he reached the height of the streetlights, he stopped, let go with his hands, and lunged into space, soaring over the milling shoppers. He spectralized just enough that with his charcoal sweatshirt and black corduroys, he was no more noticeable than a pigeon swooping overhead.

He landed on the roof of the carousel. He couldn't levitate well enough to land without a sound, but he did slow himself enough so that the light thud of his arrival was drowned out by the off-key carousel music and the laughter of its riders. Oliver leaped again, back up into the dark fog. This time he landed on the top of a long, narrow roof. It was a fountain. In the summer, water dropped from either side of this stone roof into troughs on the ground, creating a long hallway with liquid walls. There was a metal walkway beneath the roof, so that one could walk between the two sheets of water. The fountain was dry now. Skateboarders were doing jumps and slides along the stone benches on either side of it, and two people stood on the metal walkway.

Oliver peered under the roof. "Hey."

"Dah!" Dean jumped.

Emalie spun around, her face startled as well, but then she punched Dean. "Dean!" She rolled her eyes.

Oliver flipped down onto the walkway. "Hi," he said. He wasn't sure what to say next. "You got my note."

Emalie rolled her eyes. "Of course, I got it."

Oliver had left the scrap of paper wedged beneath her desk early Friday morning. "So, you brought the negative."

Emalie nodded and tapped her vest pocket. "Got it."

Oliver looked at her. Dean looked at Oliver, then at Emalie. "Emalie," Dean said.

Emalie only stood, hands in the pockets of her vest.

Oliver held out his hand. "Can I have it?"

Emalie didn't move. Dean started to fidget. "Emalie, come on." He checked his watch. "We told my parents an hour and a half."

Emalie only stared at Oliver. "We're going with you," she said.

"What?!" Dean threw his hands in the air. "Oh, great. Knew this was going to happen!"

"No," Oliver replied beneath Dean's ranting.

"Mmm," Emalie nodded.

"No!" said Oliver, feeling more flustered.

"We go, or you don't get the photo."

Dean took a few frustrated steps, his large feet clanging on the grating, then spun around. "Emalie, just give it to him!"

Oliver stared at Emalie. She stared back. Then with a shrug of the eyebrows he said, "All right." Then he turned and headed down the fountain walkway, away from them. "Fine."

"I can't believe the vampire is the one whose head is on straight," Dean muttered as they watched Oliver leave. Emalie didn't reply.

Oliver kept walking, listening to Dean and wishing, for a moment, that there was a cliff nearby, so that he could just kind of bump Dean off. Because even though Oliver looked like he was leaving, he wasn't. Emalie had one more second to give in.

Oliver reached the end of the walkway. Emalie hadn't spoken. All right then. He'd had a feeling this would happen. Shaking his head, Oliver ducked out of the walkway and climbed back to the roof of the fountain. He reappeared a moment later, walking back toward Emalie and Dean holding a large lump of fabric.

"What's that?" Dean asked.

"Put these on," Oliver said, holding out the pile.

Emalie almost smiled. She reached out and held up two hooded coats. "Here," she said, handing one to Dean.

"You have to be kidding," Dean whined.

"Just take it," commanded Emalie.

Dean did, but then his face scrunched. "It smells, like — horrible!"

"That's the point," Oliver explained. "We have to hide your scent."

Emalie began slipping on the long, hooded green coat. It was far too big for her and hung down over her hands and below her knees. As she pulled the hood up over her head, she looked like she might be sick.

"Yeah . . ." Dean was saying as he held the other jacket, a purple one, in front of him, his arms stiff. "But this seems kinda extreme."

"You think this is extreme?" Oliver said, letting a note of darkness tint his voice. "If anyone in the Underground smells a live human . . ."

"We get it," Emalie said, "Come on, Dean."

Dean rolled his eyes then reluctantly put on the coat. He had just slipped on the second sleeve when he froze. "Wait, what you just said — that means these jackets aren't from — humans?"

Oliver couldn't help but smile a little. "They're from humans, just not living ones." He started off down the walkway again.

"Oh, no . . ." Dean started grabbing at the jacket.

"Dean, relax," Emalie grabbed his arm.

"But these are — did you steal these from graves? Of course you did, you —"

"No," Oliver replied impatiently, "I didn't steal them. I bought them from two zombies over in Denny Park."

"Z —" Dean's mouth seemed to break down.

"You should be grateful," said Oliver, enjoying Dean's terror a bit. "It wasn't easy. Zombies are very possessive of their things."

"Then how did you get these?" Emalie asked.

"Well," Oliver said, turning to walk again. "There are some things that they like more."

"Don't zombies eat b . . . brains?" Dean called from behind.

Oliver ignored him. As he reached the end of the fountain walkway, he stopped in the shadows. This time, he crouched down and lifted up one of the heavy sections of metal grating beneath their feet. Emalie and

Dean reached him and looked down into a sewer drain.

"Um . . ." Dean croaked.

"Now listen," Oliver said. "Stay behind me, and no matter what happens, keep your hoods up and your heads down." He dropped out of sight.

Emalie and Dean climbed gingerly down a metal ladder. As they reached the sewer tunnel below, Oliver helped them step over to a ledge. They started forward, black water rushing beside them. In moments, the darkness became complete. Oliver felt Emalie's hand grasp the back of his jacket.

"I can't see a thing," Dean muttered.

After a minute, light began to return — a soft green light. A thin vein of neon appeared on the ceiling of the tunnel, providing more than enough light for vampire eyes, and just barely enough for human. Still, Emalie kept hold of Oliver's jacket.

They reached an intersection, lit with sconces of magmalight. Oliver turned to the wall and whispered, "*Anemoi.*" A map lit, bathing the three in sparking light.

"Wow," Emalie breathed as Oliver pinched the corners of the funnel-shaped matrix in his fingers, rotating it to get his bearings. "It's a map?" Oliver nodded. "What are these?" She pointed to the scrawled Skrit symbols.

"Those are Skrit symbols," Oliver said. "It's a vampire language."

"Mmm." Emalie's eyes were wide.

"They look like they're written in blood," Dean whispered.

Emalie reached up and touched the projection. Her finger sank through the light, and she slid it through one of the Skrit runes. "What does this one mean?" she asked. It was a spiraling shape set within a square, thicker and thinner at points, as if drawn with a brush. There was a crimson tinge to the color:

"That's the Underground Center," Oliver replied. "The boundary indicates this world. Square corners are the boundaries of matter. The spiral is the Underground. It says more than that, but I haven't learned much Skrit yet."

Emalie continued staring, fascinated. Dean stood behind her, also staring, but his look was more like a frozen computer screen.

"Come on." Oliver blew out the map, then turned and continued.

They were now walking down a major tunnel that sloped steadily downward. Its wide walls were lit with

< 110 >

sconces and adorned with ancient paintings and long tapestries. The candelabras, tucked into half-moon recesses in the floor, cast their wild shadows on the walls.

"I didn't think it would be so —" Emalie started, then paused.

"What?" asked Oliver.

"Warm. It feels warm down here," she continued. "Not just the air, but like, the light and the art, and . . ." She halted, pulling Oliver to a stop by the back of his sweatshirt. "Oh."

Oliver turned to find her staring wide-eyed at the tapestry beside them, yet the fascination in her eyes had turned cold.

"Y . . . you were saying?" Dean muttered softly.

Oliver glanced up and down the hall at the long weaving they were passing: It depicted a wide room of stone. Every few feet along the tapestry, there was a collection of hooded figures employing ancient means of torture upon shackled prisoners, involving tubs of water, ropes and weights, flames. Oliver wasn't sure which specific Inquisition it was, maybe the Spanish, but there had been so many throughout the Middle Ages, they were all kind of repetitive and blended together. The particular moment in the tapestry that had Emalie transfixed involved two children, who were being made to face a beast of some kind, something from the Underworld. Oliver wished she hadn't seen it.

"Their faces," Emalie said softly. "I've never seen anything so scared-looking, it's —" She turned away, swallowing hard.

"It's just because it's accurate," Oliver offered, trying to be helpful.

"Why would you want to show that so *accurately*?" she muttered.

"Well —"

"Let's just go," Emalie said quickly, pushing Oliver forward. He heard Dean sigh behind her. Oliver tried to think of something else to say about the images in the tapestry, about how it wasn't the *vampires* who were doing the awful things in that tapestry, but decided just to leave it.

They walked for five minutes, silent except for their footfalls. On either side, they began to see abandoned chambers: the deep, forgotten basements of buildings, with dusty piles of tables and chairs scattered about. They passed a cobwebbed storefront, a general store. There were still barrels and sacks of pioneer supplies piled inside.

"I took a tour through stuff like this once," Dean mused quietly. "There used to be bars and shops and stuff, beneath the streets."

"Those were good times to be a vampire," said Oliver, "I mean, you know, 'cause . . ." He trailed off, still feeling uncertainty from Emalie.

They turned right, then left, and finally the tunnel leveled out. Oliver began to hear the din of activity up ahead.

"How much farther is —" Dean began.

"Tsss," Oliver warned.

Two vampires were approaching: a man and woman, well dressed, hooked at the elbows. The woman carried a tiny triangular purse that was actually a cage, with a black cloth over it. Something scurried and hissed inside. The man was in the middle of a story but paused as the two groups passed. Oliver nodded to him, hoping that Dean would have the good sense to keep his head down.

"Not really the sort to be hanging around with," the man said, nose upturned at the scent of zombies.

"They're my servants," Oliver said quickly, keeping his pace brisk.

"Hmph," added the woman, and her purse rattled as if in agreement.

As they passed by, Oliver listened to make sure the couple kept walking. They did. Oliver felt Emalie grab his jacket again.

"Servants?" she hissed.

"Vampires sometimes have zombies as servants," explained Oliver. "It was the safest thing to say."

"Oh, man," Dean said hoarsely. "That was crazy. We should go back."

"Too late," Oliver said.

They'd reached the end of the sewer line. Beside them, the water continued into a dark tunnel. In front of them was a solid wall, with a wide set of platinum double doors. The same spiral-in-a-square Skrit had been etched across the seam of the doors.

"Ready?" Oliver asked, glancing back at them.

Neither replied, but Emalie nodded sternly.

Oliver pushed through the doors. They descended a long, carpeted staircase. When they reached the bottom, they found themselves standing on the edge of a bustling stream of people moving past them in both directions on a wide walkway that curved away to the left and right. The ceiling rose high above them. Well-dressed vampires, young and old, hurried along, pulling kids, arms full of bags, long coats trailing behind them.

Oliver headed directly through the jostling crowd, leading Emalie and Dean to the other side of the walkway, where they reached a stone railing that looked out on the full expanse of the Underground Center.

They were standing on a ring-shaped stone walkway, lined with shops, which encircled a huge, bottomless chasm. Looking down, they could see more ringed levels beneath them.

"How many floors are there?" Emalie whispered.

"Nine," Oliver replied.

At first glance, the Center looked like a human shopping mall, arranged in the shape of a cylinder, with gleaming stores and throngs of shoppers — yet the shops were lit with torches of fire and tubes and globes of molten magmalight. At regular intervals around the ringed levels, instead of escalators or elevators, there were only gaps. The crowds of well-dressed vampires simply walked off the edges, then levitated across, or up and down, from one level to the next. Children who had not yet mastered the forces scaled the walls like insects.

A young vampire man stepped up just beside Emalie. Without breaking stride, he hopped onto the stone railing and stepped off, levitating smoothly across the chasm to a different floor. There were other vampires out in the space, doing the same. In the center of the chasm, they veered to avoid an enormous torrent of falling water.

High above, countless sewer pipes shot out of the walls, near the high rock ceiling. The pipes crisscrossed the space, and had all been sliced open at the center. Their combined waters formed this huge cascade, which dropped down the chasm into unseen depths that were clouded by steam.

"What's down there?" Dean asked.

"The ninth level is the charion station," Oliver explained as Emalie and Dean peered over his shoulders. It wasn't entirely dark below the ninth level. There was a faint glow of red light and heat amid the steam clouds. "Below that is the Yomi," said Oliver. "That's the black market. I don't think anyone really knows how deep that goes."

"Guh," Dean muttered queasily, leaning away from the railing.

Oliver looked to Emalie, whose expression of wonder had finally returned. "I guess it's pretty amazing," he offered. "It's really nothing compared to the Underworld cities."

She nodded slightly, then looked around further, and suddenly her eyes narrowed. "Are those —" she whispered, "are those *Christmas trees?*"

Every level was dotted with festive trees, decorated with red lights, silver garlands, and glittering ornaments. Some ornaments were simply Skrit symbols fashioned from iron, but some others seemed to be moving, as if they were alive. These were tiny lizards nesting in gold cages in the trees.

"We celebrate Longest Night," said Oliver. "It's the biggest vampire holiday. Well, Festival of Waning Sun, in the fall, is almost as big, but —"

"But — how can vampires have *Christmas* trees?" For the first time, Oliver saw a look on Emalie's face that wasn't wonder or fear, but disappointment.

"Well," Oliver said, feeling a bit defensive for the first time, "Longest Night coincides with the winter solstice. I mean — vampires have been celebrating celestial holidays since before humans could even talk. Besides, those aren't technically Christmas trees. There were these Germanic tribes and Wiccans, who decorated trees for the winter solstice way before people started using them for Christmas." Oliver decided not to mention that those Germanic tribes sometimes decorated their trees with the bodies of their slaves.

Emalie gazed at him blankly. "What?"

Oliver couldn't tell whether she was intrigued or repulsed. "There's only been a Christmas for like, two thousand years," he went on. "There's been a Longest Night since the beginning of the universe."

Emalie considered this, but then she shook her head. "Christmas is about giving and love. Demons can't —"

"We love," Oliver said, and felt a surge of embarrassment. "And we give gifts, too, for Longest Night." Oliver stopped himself. There was no need to get into *what* those gifts were. He thought about what to tell her next. There was one choice fact that Emalie might enjoy. "Do you really think," said Oliver, "that the only reason the original Santa Claus snuck into human homes was to leave them presents?"

"Santa Claus is only a story," Dean said, sounding like a sad child.

Oliver only shrugged.

"All right," Emalie said finally, with an almost-smile. "What do you mean?"

"Think about it." Oliver relaxed a bit, seeing that he was starting to win Emalie back over. "The presents, the legends, the costume. It's a small price to pay for being invited into thousands of human homes."

"You're saying that he's not human," said Emalie. Oliver raised his eyebrows. "Okay, we get it." She glared at him, but the spark had returned to her eyes. "Where is Dead Désirée's?"

Oliver nodded. "Third floor, come on."

Emalie took hold of Oliver's coat again as he merged back into the crowd. They passed the windows of clothing stores, where live models were dressed in fashionable outfits of leather and Gore-Tex; a luggage store featuring coffin trunks; several candy and cake confectioners; a skin and tooth care store where a white-coated man was bending over a customer, demonstrating the latest nano-diamond stiletto tooth file; an oil portrait studio . . .

Every now and then, Emalie's or Dean's gaze would cause them to stray from the line behind Oliver, and they would be jostled by passing vampires. "Heads down," Oliver hissed. His nerves were fraying, but luckily, the vampires were busy, and zombies, as a rule, weren't worth noticing.

Oliver kept his gaze ahead, yet every now and then he was drawn to passing faces. Some looked down with disdain at his smelly companions, scowling at Oliver for being in such company. Yet others seemed to only look at Oliver. One woman's face lit with recognition, but Oliver didn't think he'd ever seen her before. Once, a man tugged his friend's jacket and pointed in Oliver's direction as they passed. He didn't know why anyone would recognize him and he didn't think this had ever happened before. Then again, he'd never been watching nervously to see if people noticed him before. It was possible that they thought he was wealthy, and the zombies were his servants, though not *really* wealthy, because zombies, as a rule, weren't very reliable. But then there was that old man at the doctor's office who recognized him as well.

These moments of attention were making him too nervous. Emalie and Dean really had no idea what Oliver had gotten them into. Since they entered the center, he'd been trying to figure out how he would get them out if they were discovered. He had yet to come up with a solution.

They passed through a wide space in the crowd by

the food court. Emalie strayed hard as she eyed the restaurants: There were fast-food stops, like Berthold's, which served many varieties of insects and small creatures in suspension; Xanadu's, with its thirty-seven different animal flavors of blood sorbet; a trendy shish kebab place called All Things Rodent; and the smoky, torch-lit booths of *L'organo Sanguinante*, where families and couples sat for fine dining. Oliver sped up, and as he did so, he heard a strange clicking sound in the din. It distracted him momentarily, as he tried to place the sound.

Now they reached the first gap in the floors. Oliver quickly pulled Emalie and Dean to the wall. Kids spidered around them, climbing up and down. "Grab my shoulders," he said, placing his hands against the rock wall, "and don't let go."

"This is so not good," Dean said, shaking.

"Just grab him," Emalie ordered. She locked her elbow around Oliver's upper arm. Oliver stepped up onto the wall. His foot slipped, and he wobbled for a moment. This was a lot of weight, a lot of concentration.

"Dude, dude, dude," Dean whispered nervously.

"Tsss!" Oliver hissed icily. Dean managed to stop speaking, but his heavy breathing was relentless in Oliver's ear. He stepped to the right, then slowly scaled down the wall. The shoulders and bags of passing vampires brushed Emalie and Dean. Their grips tightened. Oliver focused only on his hands and the wall, until he felt the floor of the third level against his feet.

They rejoined the crowds and walked another minute, until they reached their destination. A sign in understated neon script read:

Dead Désirée's Drug & Alchemy Emporium

Oliver quickly led them inside.

CHAPTER 9

Dead Désirée

As Oliver and his zombie imposters stepped through a revolving glass door, they found themselves in a stark, brightly lit store. Neat rows of orderly shelves stretched away from them. As the door slid shut, it extinguished all the hustling, bustling sounds of the center, leaving them in near silence. Tinny music drifted distantly from speakers in the ceiling. It sounded human: a mellow bossa nova. The store was very still. A pale, almost color-less magmalight gleamed from long tubes in the ceiling. The entire store seemed washed in white so bright that it made Oliver squint, and yet, a dark, grimy green lingered in the corners and shadows. The air was humid and tinged with a strong smell of ammonia, like the floors had just been cleaned.

Oliver led them down the center aisle. The floor looked tiled, but their footsteps made no sound. They passed among rows of black glass bottles and small wooden boxes. Everything was marked in white Skrit labels, what they contained a mystery for the most part, even to Oliver.

"This place doesn't seem very vampirelike," Dean whispered.

"Désirée's not a vampire," said Oliver over his shoulder.

"Then what is she?"

"Something more dangerous."

"W . . . well can you be more specific?"

Oliver shrugged. "Nobody really knows what she is."

"But —"

"Tsss."

They'd reached the end of the aisle, and found themselves at a high counter. A narrow woman in a pristine white lab coat stood with her back to them. Her crimson hair was tied back in a bun. "Just a moment," she said before Oliver had a chance to speak. She stood perfectly still, gazing into a diamond-shaped mirror with a frame made of jade. Oliver was too low to see any reflection of her in it, seeing instead only the glowing white ceiling lights.

He took the opportunity to turn quickly to Emalie and Dean. He tried to show them in a single glance that here there was even more danger than in the crowd they'd just left. He should have given them more of a warning about her, but it was too late now.

"Now then, how can I help you, Oliver?"

Oliver turned back to find Désirée looking down at him pleasantly. Her face was plaster white. She wore thin glasses. On first glance, she looked delicate and pretty. Oliver was surprised that she knew his name, but then reminded himself that he shouldn't have been. Désirée was known to have *sight*. There was much debate as to what Désirée actually was, but no one questioned it too much, mostly because it was rumored that Désirée didn't appreciate such questions, and as nearly everyone needed something from her, no one wanted to upset her.

Now she looked over Oliver's hooded companions. When her eyes moved back to Oliver, they seemed to gleam with understanding. Still, all she did was smile. "A photo experiment, is it?"

Oliver found that his throat was tight. "That's right."

"I thought your parents told you not to play with cameras?" Her smile broadened and, as it did, Oliver noticed something odd about Désirée's face. It seemed like when she moved, it took her skin a second to catch up. In fact, it was almost as if her *real* face were *beneath* this white plaster front, moving on its own, and that the face they could see was only a mask that could barely keep up. Oliver felt like behind Désirée's pleasant smile, there was a wider grin, with darker teeth. Like behind her mild lavender eyes, there was perhaps a different set of eyes entirely.

"Yes, they told me that," Oliver answered. He figured it was no use lying to her.

"And yet you want to develop this photo anyway? Interesting," Désirée purred. "Curious about what remains out of focus, aren't you?"

"I . . . I just want to see it."

"Is that all?" Désirée's head swiveled slightly, and lumps seemed to move beneath her mask, as if whatever was below was rolling about, enjoying the lies. "Wouldn't you say that you're looking for a bit more than that?"

Oliver shrugged. "Sure. I . . . I guess."

"Well, good." Désirée nodded. "I, for one, think it would have been best for you to know long before now."

"Know what?" Oliver asked.

Désirée's face slowly lost its smile. "What you want to find out." Before Oliver could reply, she spun around and stalked off into the shelves of medicines. "I have just the thing, of course."

"She's not normal," Dean muttered.

"Tsss," Oliver hissed. Suddenly, he heard that muted clicking sound again, and here in the silence of Désirée's, he recognized what it was. He turned, and out of the corner of his eye, saw Emalie holding open her jacket ever-so-slightly —

Oliver spun and caught her hand before she could snap another photo with her camera, which she had hanging around her neck.

"Don't," Oliver said icily. "No more."

Emalie's face drained. "I —"

"You'll get us killed."

Emalie slid her jacket closed, face pale. "I wouldn't have gotten caught," she muttered stubbornly.

"Now then . . ."

Oliver turned to find Désirée emerging from the shelves. Her smile took a moment to stretch back to life. She placed a black bottle on the table, labeled with a white rune. This Skrit had an odd-angled, diamond border. It indicated another world, yet Oliver wasn't sure which. He was pretty sure that diamonds meant higher worlds, yet the angles and lengths of sides were unique to each one, and his class hadn't studied those yet.

Oliver looked up to find Désirée looking over his shoulder again. Her face had lost a little of its grin. Now she looked back to him. "Interesting, Oliver, indeed. Found yourself an Orani, did you?"

"A what?" Oliver asked, though he thought he recognized the word.

"One who sees." Désirée nodded toward Emalie. "Though she doesn't know it, yet." Désirée looked back to Oliver. "I guess you're no stranger to taking risks."

"What do you mean?" Oliver asked.

Désirée's grin returned in full, the skin stretching tight, but she didn't answer. Instead, she opened the black bottle and tapped one drop onto her finger. It was a silver liquid, thick like glue, yet it immediately began to dissolve into the air.

"You'll want to apply this to the negative before you print the photo," Désirée explained. "It will correct for the error. And make sure your — *friends* — wear gloves."

Oliver nodded. "But what do you mean *error*?"

"Human film reacts when it's exposed to light," Désirée said smoothly. "Humans then develop the film so that they can see the visible light spectrum. There are, of course, other spectra that humans know nothing about and would never know to develop. This tincture will bring out those spectra."

"So this is what a vampire would use to develop their photo?"

Désirée's smile broadened more than ever. "Why, Oliver, no. This is what *you* need to develop *your* photo."

"W . . . what?"

"You'll understand soon enough, won't you? Now . . ." Désirée slid the bottle toward him, then reached into her pocket. "I have one more thing for you." She produced a large crimson crystal, set in a silver diamond of metal and hanging from a chain.

"What's that?"

Désirée held it out to him. "Just an amulet of Ephyra, for protection. Maybe you've realized by now that you're entering into a more dangerous world." Her eyes flashed over his shoulder again. "I would advise you to wear this at all times."

Oliver took the amulet. He gazed at the crimson crystal, yet it had no reflection, no shine even. It seemed to absorb the light, and there was the faintest burning glow from its center.

"Around your neck, dear," Désirée offered with grandmotherly concern. Oliver slipped the chain over his head. "Now run along, before the hour gets too early."

"Okay. Thanks." Oliver reached into his pocket. "How much for this?"

"Five for the tincture," Désirée replied. "The amulet is my gift to you."

"All right." Oliver slapped a five-*myna* square on the counter, then turned to leave.

"Oliver." He found Désirée with her hands out in front of her, fingers touching. "I do hope you'll come again if you need to."

"Okay," Oliver said.

"Because you'll need to." Désirée grinned.

Oliver headed out faster then they'd come in. His thoughts were spinning, but more than anything, he just wanted to get out of Désirée's. He led the way through the revolving door, into the bustling crowd. They made their way back to the gap and up the wall, no one speaking. They were passing the food court, when Emalie stopped again, pulling Oliver's coat, and causing Dean to bump into the two of them. Oliver spun to find Emalie pulling out her camera.

"Stop it," he muttered, squeezing her arm.

Emalie winced, but shot him a defiant look. "Come on! We're almost home free, there's nothing wrong with —"

"Oliver!"

Oliver froze. He looked out across the food court. There, standing up from a table, was Theo. Sitting on either side of him were Brent and Maggots, all with full baskets from Berthold's.

Now Theo's face narrowed with suspicion. "What's up, buddy?" he called.

Oliver turned, grabbed Emalie and Dean by their sleeves, and started into the crowd. From behind him, he heard Theo announce, "Dude's gone from cows to zombies." Oliver glanced over his shoulder, and his view of Theo was obscured by the throng.

"Come on! Hurry!" he urged, dragging Emalie and Dean toward the exit doors. He glanced over his shoulder again —

And bumped right into Theo. "What's up, Ollie?" Theo asked.

Oliver looked around, panicking, as Brent and Maggots flanked them on either side.

Chapter 10

Chasm

Oliver felt like his universe had shrunk to a small bubble, its walls formed by the crowd pulsing by on either side. Here in the space between, Oliver stood, with his vampire classmates in front of him, and behind him were his — what? What were Emalie and Dean? Conspirators? *Friends?* But it really didn't matter, did it? All that mattered was that they were human.

"What are you doing here with *them*?" Theo nodded to what he thought were zombies. Emalie and Dean kept their heads down, faces hidden by their hoods. Emalie was still holding the back of Oliver's sweatshirt, and he could feel her hand shaking slightly.

Oliver didn't know how to answer. "Get out of my way, guys," he said, and tried to step through them —

But Brent and Maggots fell in tight on either side of Theo. "No," Theo said simply. "Not until you explain why you're walking around with a couple of stinking zombies."

"Gross," said Maggots, sniffing the air in an exaggerated fashion. His brow scrunched quizzically, and he scratched at his head.

"I don't have to explain," Oliver muttered, trying the strong and silent routine, but he didn't feel strong, and his insides were screaming. "Why don't you guys go annoy someone else?"

"Ha," Theo smirked, "actually, Oliver, *you're* the one who's annoying. I guess you didn't hear." His eyes flashed. "Wait, I get it. These are your new friends. That makes sense. Why didn't I see it coming? First, you're getting your picture taken by a —"

"Human," Maggots mumbled.

"Yeah," Theo continued, "And now —"

"No." Maggots nudged Theo hard in the arm. "Humans."

"Dude," Brent chimed in, "why are you talking about —"

"Wait —" Theo cut him off. He sniffed the air, looking confused for a moment as well.

Oliver watched, helpless. He had to get out of here. But they'd never make it back to the sewers, and even if they did, Emalie and Dean weren't fast enough, not even close.

"Oh, no way!" Theo said. His face stretched in an amazed smile, and his eyes momentarily glowed pale blue. He looked triumphantly at Oliver. "Wow, Oliver. You're in so much trouble."

"What?" Brent almost whined.

"Duh," Maggots elbowed him, then pointed past Oliver. "Humans," he muttered.

Just the word caused a passing woman to turn in shock, shaking her head as if questioning what she'd just heard. She kept walking, but Theo had seen her pause. Now he raised his arm.

"Don't," Oliver said miserably, "Theo —"

"Humans!" Theo called flatly. He didn't sound malicious, like they were just a couple of kids messing around or playing a joke; he sounded like he was stating an important, disturbing fact. "Humans!" he called again.

The entire crowd began to slow and turn, and immediately, others picked out the scent. Oliver knew the zombie jackets were strong enough if you weren't *looking* for humans, but if you were. . . .

Now Maggots joined Theo. "Humans!" They announced together.

"Impossible," an adult said amid the grumbling crowd. Suddenly, someone snatched the hood off of Emalie's head.

A gasp seemed to silence the entire Underground. Dean's hood was pulled off as well. Everyone was coming to a stop, bumping into one another as they turned their heads.

Oliver watched it all happening, and knew there was nothing he could say, nothing he could do, except —

He grabbed Emalie and Dean by their arms and slammed sideways through the stopping confusion of people. "Hold on to me!" he shouted. They were both too scared to reply, but he felt their grips tightening on his arms and digging into his shoulders as he burst through the surprised crowd, vaulted onto the stone railing, then leaped into the chasm.

There was a chorus of shocked and surprised voices, then the rush of air drowned out everything. They sailed down from the top floor, and in moments, Oliver knew that there was no way he could control their fall. He concentrated hard, trying to hold on to the forces. It was no use. His grip was already slipping. They were picking up speed —

But he could maneuver them a little, and so he arced toward the nearest levitating vampire, slamming into him in midair.

"What the —" the older gentleman grunted.

For a moment, they became a tangle of four bodies, but then the adult righted himself and the group's fall slowed. Oliver was hanging on to the man's shoulder, with Emalie and Dean hanging on to both of his. The man eyed Oliver and the humans with confusion, but then his face began to darken demonically.

"What do we have here?" He clawed at the humans.

But Oliver was already vaulting away, pushing hard off the man. They sailed upward for a moment, then began to fall again, plunging down two more levels, and landing on a large woman who was floating serenely, a raven perched on her shoulder.

"What!?" she bellowed. The raven flapped free of her shoulder, and the foursome careened into the torrent of falling water in the center of the chasm. They were immediately soaked and wrapped in the water's roar. The woman's hat was lost, and her gray hair matted down over her snarling face. "How dare you!" This woman was very strong. Despite their tangle and the force of the water, Oliver could feel her holding the group's descent at a reasonable speed. Now she somehow got a hand free and reached wildly for Dean. Her nails raked across his arm.

"Ahh!" Dean shouted.

"Twisted boy!" the woman scolded, water rolling down her bloated face. "But I'll take the snack!"

Oliver struggled to keep her at bay, while at the same time trying to get his feet onto her to lunge away. He ended up kicking her hard in the stomach.

"Bah!" the woman groaned. "You're a miserable excuse for our kind!"

Their tangle of bodies flew free of the waterfall. Oliver was just getting himself righted when he felt a searing pain in his shoulder. "Gah!" The raven was already flying away, having left a deep puncture in Oliver's shoulder. He could hear it clucking as it circled around for more.

"I'm going to —" the woman started.

But Oliver finally planted his feet and launched them away with all the strength he could muster. They arced across the chasm. In a dizzying blur, Oliver saw the lowest levels of the Underground and the deep crimson glow from below. They were entering the steam clouds now. If this jump didn't work . . .

Suddenly, they were tumbling onto hard rock. Oliver found himself on his back, staring up at the underside of the lowest platform of the Underground. He could see heads peering over the edges of the railings in different spots, but he could also see others levitating across the chasm, business as usual. Oliver looked around to see that they were on a carved stone ledge. Steam clouds crawled along the walls. A cave led into darkness behind them.

"Uh," Emalie groaned. Oliver sat up to find Emalie on her knees, rubbing her arm.

"Are you all right?" he asked.

She grimaced, but then began moving her arm up and down. Her face twitched, and she opened her zombie coat — to find her camera broken. The lens was cracked, and film was spilling out of the back. "It was my mom's," she said with a sigh, then muttered, "I'm fine." She looked at Oliver. "What would have happened to us up there?"

Oliver stood up, brushing himself off. "You don't want to know." He checked his pocket and was relieved to find the glass bottle intact. "We need to get out of here."

Emalie stood. She looked at him severely.

"I'm sorry," Oliver said.

"No." Emalie shook her head. "It would have been my fault, if —" She shook a little, and now started crying quietly.

Oliver had no idea what to do. Crying wasn't something that he'd ever had to deal with before.

"I made you bring us, I —" Emalie balled her hands into tight fists, staring at the ground. She held her breath for a long minute, then shook it off.

Oliver waited a second. "We should go," he said again.

Emalie nodded.

"Whoa." Oliver turned to find Dean standing at the edge of the ledge, looking down. Oliver and Emalie joined him. The chasm still dropped into darkness, but the red glow was more apparent. Bare rock walls dropped another hundred feet, and then there were more ledges. The view was obscured by steam, but they could just make out more caves leading away from the chasm, lit by red and lavender lights. They could clearly hear the din of many voices, and much activity. The sound was different than in the mall above. This was rougher somehow, darker. There was the harsh clinking of metal. The rumble of primitive machinery, the echo of a deep drum . . .

"That's the Yomi?" Dean whispered.

"Yeah," Oliver said quietly.

There was a particularly loud crash, and also the sound of tinny music.

"W . . . what's it like?" Dean asked.

"It's pretty Old World," Oliver said. "Kind of lawless. There are vampires who live there and never come to the surface. Zombies and wraiths, too." Oliver had never been to the Yomi. The thought of it actually made him a bit nervous. Just being a vampire wasn't enough to ensure safety down there. "Come on," he said.

They walked away from the ledge and headed into the cavern. A low rock ceiling arced over them. The dark space around them widened, and a pale yellow light increased. They reached a cobblestone walkway and followed it.

"Put your hoods back up," Oliver instructed. Emalie and Dean quickly did so. They emerged from darkness onto what looked like a subway train platform. Its walls blinked with flashing video screens that were so thin they hung like cloth. Beside the platform was a large, clear tube. Vampires stood about, alone and in families, waiting patiently, some with luggage at their sides.

Oliver led them quickly along the platform, weaving in and out of the throng, who were eyeing the tube expectantly. Now, the floor and walls began to shake. "Ow," Dean whispered. Oliver could feel it, too. The pressure was changing, lowering, making his ears ache.

"A charion is coming," Oliver said matter-of-factly.

There was a rush of air and a low humming sound, so low that it vibrated their teeth. Oliver paused and steadied his balance. A blast of air overwhelmed the tunnel, and the clear tube shook. A cylindrical train shot into the station, halting immediately, creating a wicked backdraft of air. The humming quickly cycled down to silence. Segments of the clear tube slid open. The charion was black, and smoking. Large, glowing embers, still smoldering, tumbled down the sides. Massive fans rumbled to life in the station, sucking up the dark smoke and ash that billowed from the train.

The charion doors slid open, and the trio just caught a glimpse of the plush, low-lit interior before passengers started crowding off and on. There were deep seats and long plasma screens showing advertisements and views of the towering spires of far-off Underworld cities. Gentle string music hummed lightly. Above each seat hung a network of red tubing, with brass valves at the end. The valves were numbered and corresponded to a menu etched on the arm of each seat.

"That train goes to the Underworld?" Dean whispered.

Oliver nodded and continued to lead them along the wall of the platform, blending in with the people heading off the train and up a long hallway.

"What are —"

"Tsss." Oliver silenced Dean. There was no time for explanations right now, especially about those red dining tubes. Still, it was all Oliver could do to keep them moving. He loved the charions and loved traveling, maybe more than anything else. He didn't really care where the train was going, just that it *was* going, with the world passing by outside. *You should just get on right now,* he thought wildly. Take Emalie and Dean and just go somewhere where they wouldn't be in danger. Except it was fifteen hours to New York City, twenty hours to Shanghai. In that amount of time, his disappearance would easily be discovered. *At least, you'd have those fifteen hours,* he thought glumly. Given what had just happened in the center, his existence might be over as soon as he got home.

They walked up a curving tunnel, then entered an enormous central station. Vampires streamed in and out of tunnels to charions heading in all directions, stood in lines to purchase tickets from antique booths, and crowded around standing tables at a café in the center of the station.

"Wow," Emalie breathed, daring to gaze up at the dizzyingly high dome ceiling. On it was a dazzling route map. Magmalight lines connected brilliant gold etchings of surface and the Underworld cities around the world.

Oliver didn't pause to explain any of it. He pressed forward, across the cavernous room and straight toward a row of gold elevator doors. These went express to and from the surface. Doors slid open and closed, vampires crowding on and off as bells sounded.

Oliver hung back, waiting for the timing to provide a fairly empty elevator car, and then ushered the humans in. The elevator shot up with another earsplitting pressure change. Moments later, they were disembarking in an abandoned Seattle bus tunnel. It was cold, damp, and colorless, save for a few bare lightbulbs. Oliver felt a bit of disappointment mixed with his relief to be back on the surface. He led them up two nonworking escalators, then a set of crumbling stairs, and finally out through an iron gate.

They were back downtown, among the human holiday shoppers. Oliver took the coats from Emalie and Dean. They both looked around blankly. "You should get back," Oliver said.

This snapped them out of it. Dean checked his watch. "Okay, right. Yeah, we're a couple of minutes late — not bad. My parents should still be over at the Santa photos with my brother and sister," he said, then added, "guess I shouldn't spoil it for them."

Emalie looked seriously at Oliver. "What are you going to do?"

Oliver wasn't sure. He hadn't thought that far ahead. Now that he did, he realized that what had just happened may well have already gotten back to his parents. The vampire community wasn't *that* big, and a story about a vampire child taking humans into the Underground would spread fast. Anyone who knew his parents would feel obligated to tell them. "I don't know," he said. "I think I'm going to be in trouble." Trouble wasn't the half of it. He had no idea how his parents and brother were going to react. Not to mention what was going to happen in school on Monday.

Emalie seemed to read his thoughts. "We should do the photo tonight. Before —"

"Yeah," Oliver agreed. If they didn't do it now, he might never have the chance.

Emalie turned purposefully to Dean. Oliver was impressed that her decisive self had returned so quickly. "Dean, we'll ask your parents if you can sleep over."

"Right," Dean said with a sigh, like he didn't have the energy to protest.

"Come over after midnight," Emalie said to Oliver.

Oliver nodded. "See you there."

Emalie nodded back.

"Emalie, let's go," urged Dean, and pulled her into the crowd.

Oliver stepped back into the shadows on the side of the building, spectralized, then climbed up the wall into darkness. He moved to the edge of the building and watched as Emalie and Dean bobbed away through the crowd, safe in the world of cheery holiday light. He almost wished he could go with them. Because going home was not an option. Whatever might be waiting for him there, he at least wanted to finish this business with the photograph before he took his punishment.

Emalie and Dean disappeared into the blur of people. Oliver retreated into the shadows, to kill time alone, until later in the night.

CHAPTER 11

An Image Revealed

Oliver made his way across town, staying out of the sewers and avoiding popular vampire spots like the stone troll, the roller coaster at Seattle Center, or any of the parks and ball fields. He hadn't told his parents where he would be all evening. Since it was a Saturday, he didn't need to, but Phlox probably expected him home for lunch around midnight. And missing that wouldn't really be a big deal, unless of course his parents knew about the incident at the Underground. If they did, then they might even be out looking for him now. He kept under the trees, wary of bats or owls that might be occupied. And if his parents somehow didn't know, then he'd still need to be home by dinner, but not before.

As he walked along, Oliver took a moment to gaze at the amulet around his neck. So far, it had not seemed to provide any protection. Of course, Désirée hadn't mentioned what kind of protection it offered. And who exactly did he need protection from? *You need protection from yourself,* thought Oliver darkly. After all, he was the one who'd gotten his photo taken, who brought humans into the Underground.

Just after midnight, he headed for Emalie's house. The upstairs was silent, the basement dark. Oliver circled around to the door and silently let himself inside. He weaved through the boxes, but paused just before he reached Emalie's darkroom space.

"I'm here," Oliver murmured.

"Wha!" There was a thud as Dean's head hit a shelf.

"Shhhh!" Emalie hissed.

The red light flicked on. Emalie was getting up from a sleeping bag that had been laid out on the floor. Dean was rubbing his head. "Man, you're quiet," he muttered, still eyeing Oliver with a bit of mistrust.

"Come on," Emalie said seriously. "Before my dad wakes up. Not that he will."

"I think he's down for the count," Dean offered. He sounded like he was trying to be sympathetic. Oliver watched Emalie for a reaction, but she didn't have one.

Oliver stepped beside her at the counter by the sink. Dean peered over their shoulders. Oliver produced the slim black bottle. The cap had a dropper, which Oliver squeezed as he lifted it off. Emalie held the negative between her fingers.

"You see the spot?" she asked quietly.

"Yeah." Oliver squeezed a tiny drop of the shimmering silver liquid onto the blurry form in the right side of the negative. There was a slight hiss of steam as the liquid seemed to evaporate. In a moment, it was gone. The negative looked the same.

"That's it?" Dean asked.

"I think so." Oliver shrugged.

"Let's see if it worked," Emalie said, and slid the negative into the top of the enlarger. A metal arm held the negative beneath a lightbulb, suspended over a white surface, where Emalie placed a blank sheet of photo paper. She flicked a switch, sending a beam of normal light through the negative and onto the paper. After a moment, she turned it off, then moved the paper into the sink, dropping it into the first tray of liquid.

The three bent over the sink. Outlines of the abandoned room began to appear. The fine diamond shapes of the chandelier seemed to sketch themselves into existence . . . and now in the area where Oliver should have been, the outline of a figure began to emerge. Oliver could see the vaguest impression of a face. Inside, he started to sag. After all this, he was about to simply see a photo of himself.

But then that area of the photo began to glow instead of darken. There was a silver light emanating from the page.

"Um," Emalie began. Oliver glanced up to her, but she wasn't looking at the photo; she had turned toward him.

Now Oliver sensed it, too. Crimson light. He looked down. A deep glow was brightening inside his sweatshirt. Oliver reached inside and produced the amulet of Ephyra. The crystal was burning from within, the light growing brighter and brighter.

"Guys, the photo," Dean said hoarsely.

Silver light was rising from the paper where Oliver should have been, creating a swirling beam shooting straight up out of the liquid. The entire room was being lit in silver now, but also in crimson, as the amulet grew brighter as well.

"What's happening?" Dean asked, his voice shaking.

There was a sound of rushing wind. The silver and crimson lights became so bright that details of the room began to wash away. Oliver looked back at the photo, and, as he did so, there was a blinding flash. Oliver lost track of sight, sound — of the entire world around him.

❉

The next thing he saw was darkness, spotted with lights. Oliver tried to move, wondering how long he'd been knocked out, but he couldn't seem to control his arms or legs. Now he could see that the lights were those of a Christmas tree, an enormous one. There were the sides of buildings and the night sky. He was looking up and moving. The Christmas tree was passing by. Then it stopped.

And she appeared. The teacher from that old chorus photo. Young, alive — human. Only she was dressed differently, wearing a wool coat with the collar upturned and a round fur hat. But it was her smile, above all else, that Oliver felt sure he recognized. She looked down at him tenderly. Her smile made him feel warm, safe. It was like nothing he'd ever felt before, and yet it seemed so familiar.

Now another face appeared, a man, gazing down at Oliver from behind the woman. He smiled slightly, then glanced around and checked his watch. His mouth moved like he was saying something to the woman, but there was still no sound. Now the woman spoke to Oliver. He watched her mouth move, then she leaned in and kissed him.

Mother, *he thought with a warm certainty, but that didn't make any sense.*

The woman disappeared, and the world began to move again. The Christmas tree slid out of view. Raindrops began to hit his face. Oliver could feel them. Cold, biting sensations. The world stopped moving again, and the woman appeared beside him. She was fiddling with an umbrella, but then she stopped. She *was looking over her shoulder. Now Oliver saw the man rush by his view, looking confused. There was a commotion —*

Then the world spun. The buildings turned sideways. Oliver was falling over. Bricks appeared beneath him, but then he was caught by hands. And lifted. His mother's face appeared again —

No, this was Phlox's face. Wait, yes, that made sense. She was his mother. Here she was smiling at him with her same look of love — only Oliver felt different. He felt terrified. And there was Sebastian's face as well, but what was on his lips? It was . . .

Phlox's smile widened, and now she leaned toward Oliver, as if to kiss him. Except then he felt a bright, searing pain. Oliver's world spun once more. There was a moment of pure white, and then Oliver found himself looking down on the scene he'd just been in: an overturned baby carriage; a woman, Phlox, crouched over a baby in her arms; Sebastian standing beside her, hand on her shoulder; and the baby was screaming, but then not. Its face became still. Its eyes slipped closed, and for a moment, a faint veil of mist seemed to circle around it, then vanish. Phlox stood, holding the unmoving baby, wrapped in a yellow blanket, only now with two red marks on its tiny neck. She handed the baby to Sebastian, who tucked it carefully into his long coat. They shared an embrace, looking down at the tiny child with tender smiles, and then stole off into the night.

Oliver rose higher. The carriage was not far from the Christmas tree, and beneath its wide branches — were two figures, lying on the pavement, unmoving.

"Oh . . ." Oliver heard a voice say breathlessly. He turned —

Emalie was floating beside him, also staring down at the scene. She was crying. Oliver looked back, but now he was rising faster, the Christmas tree shrinking, the buildings sliding past. The night started to fade into fog, its color draining as crimson light overwhelmed his vision. . . .

✸

Oliver opened his eyes and saw the cobwebbed rafters of Emalie's basement ceiling.

A face appeared above him.

"Hey!" Dean reached down and shook Oliver by the shoulder. "What happened?"

"I —" Oliver started.

"What did you do?" Dean said accusingly.

"What?" Oliver said, sitting up and blinking hard. As he did so, Dean turned and lunged to his knees beside Emalie, who was also lying flat out on the floor.

"Emalie," Dean urged, shaking her shoulder. "Come on, hey, come on!"

Suddenly, Emalie shuddered. "Gah!" She sat right up. "What happened?"

"It was that amulet!" Dean said, pointing toward Oliver. "There was this flash of light and both of you collapsed. Then you were just lying there!"

Oliver looked down to find the amulet still around his neck, but the crystal was shattered. Bits still remained in the silver casing, but the rest lay in shards in his lap and on the floor.

"It wasn't for protection," Emalie said.

Oliver looked at her. She'd been there with him, for sure. "No," he agreed, feeling a deep ache inside.

"What are you talking about?" Dean asked, his head whipping back and forth between them.

"We saw something," Emalie said carefully. She looked at Oliver to continue.

But Oliver wasn't quite sure what to say. What *had* they just seen? *You know,* he thought to himself, his anxiety flaring hotter than ever. *You know exactly what you saw.*

"The amulet was a portal of some kind," Oliver said, holding the hollow casing in his hand. He'd heard and read about such things. The alchemy involved in uncoupling from this world's time continuum, then traveling to a different moment, was very advanced. "We saw the past," Oliver continued. But it hadn't been just that. He had also *felt* the past . . . been connected to it.

Who could engineer a portal that powerful? Well, Désirée for one.

"What did you see?" Dean asked urgently.

"We saw —" Emalie started, but she caught herself and again nodded toward Oliver.

Just say it, he thought miserably. "It was my parents. . . . My human parents."

Emalie and Dean just looked at him. Oliver swallowed and pressed on. "We saw — They were killed by vampires, and —" Oliver couldn't believe what he was saying — "and I was *sired.* I was human, and — they turned me . . ."

"But isn't that how all vampires are made?" asked Dean.

Oliver shook his head, staring at the floor. "Not anymore. Not for a long time. We're all . . . *they're* all created from their parents. It's not even *possible* to sire a child. It's not supposed to be, anyway."

"But it happened to you," Dean finished.

"Not necessarily," Oliver said. "I mean, the vision might have been a trick, a lie —"

"It was real," Emalie said softly. "I could tell, I mean, I could feel that it really happened. You used to be human, Oliver. And your parents, they loved you, they . . ." Her eyes started to well up again.

Oliver was surprised by how much the vision had affected Emalie. Come to think of it, he was surprised that she had been part of it at all. But Désirée had said that Emalie had sight, so at least one thing Désirée said seemed to be true. And he agreed with Emalie, about the vision, too. As much as he wanted to believe that it might have been a trick, a lie of some kind, he knew it had been real. In a way, for as confused as he now felt, he almost felt a little better. There *was* something wrong with him, and it wasn't anything he'd done. He *was* different than everyone around him. He'd been lied to all his life. How many people knew? But who cared? His parents knew, that was enough. Not only did they know, they had stolen him from his rightful parents, his parents who had loved him, just like Emalie said. *But don't your vampire parents love you now?* Yes, they did — but not enough to tell him the truth about his origin. Not enough to help him understand why he felt different, or tell him why he needed special doctor's appointments.

Oliver sat on Emalie's floor, the thoughts swirling. He sensed Emalie standing up and turning to the sink, then sitting back down. When he looked over to her, she was holding up the photo. It was burned through, a gaping hole where the blur of Oliver had been.

"So," Dean began, "I know I wasn't in the vision, and all that" — he sounded hurt — "but what's the problem? I mean, if you're a vampire, you're not supposed to care if you were sired or made or what, right?"

"But my parents have been lying to me," Oliver said. He explained what his parents had told him, which was the same as what everyone in the vampire world believed about kids. He also told them about the doctor's visits.

Emalie seemed to be thinking hard. "Is there anything else?" she asked. "I mean, you said you heard the doctor say that you'd been chosen for something, right? And that you're being prepared for it?"

"Yeah, I think so."

"Do you know anything else about what that could be?"

"No, but . . . there's a file," Oliver said, thinking it through. "A file about my doctor's visits that my dad has. And he's supposed to show it to the people he works with."

"It probably says something about what they're doing to you," Dean added.

"We should get it," Emalie said. "Do you know where it would be?"

"He'd probably keep it in the filing cabinet in the study," Oliver guessed. He was about to say that he could look at it on his own, that once again, it would be far too dangerous to have Emalie and Dean involved. Yet he found that he wanted them to be there. Having Emalie see the portal vision had helped Oliver to believe that what he'd seen was true. He couldn't do this alone, and Emalie and Dean were a part of it all now.

"I'll get word to you of when we can meet up to check my dad's files," Oliver said, then his voice fell. "Except I don't know what's going to happen when I get home tonight. If my parents know about the Underground, you might never even see me again."

"Well," Emalie said, "don't let on that you know anything, if you can. And we'll, um, we'll just hope we hear from you." She nodded as she said it.

The three of them sat silently for a moment. "I should go," Oliver said, getting up and turning toward the door.

"Oliver." Oliver turned back to find Emalie standing. "I'm sorry, about your parents."

Oliver nodded. "Yeah." Then he disappeared into the darkness, not making a sound as he left.

CHAPTER 12

The Secret File

As Oliver wound up the spiral staircase toward the kitchen, he could hear silverware and goblets clinking on the table. He walked slowly. Either they knew, or they didn't. He passed through the empty kitchen toward the dining room. Now he heard quiet conversation between Phlox and Sebastian.

"We received the invitation today. I think it will be nice," Phlox was saying.

"What time?" Sebastian asked.

Oliver paused at the entrance to the dining room. He could see Sebastian's back. Phlox was to his left. Bane was slouched at the far end of the table. Across from Phlox was an empty chair for Oliver. He thought about turning around and taking off. How could he just sit down and pretend that this was his family? *It is your family*, he thought. But it hadn't always been. *Doesn't matter, it's the only family you have now*. This thought didn't make Oliver feel any better. Maybe he would just skip dinner —

"Hey, Ollie." Phlox was looking up . . . and smiling. "We were wondering when you'd show up." Sebastian turned with a half-smile. Bane didn't bother looking up. So far, everything was normal, which gave Oliver no choice but to sit down.

"What were you up to today?" Sebastian asked as Oliver pulled his chair up to the table.

"Nothing," Oliver said, head down.

Bane snorted to himself. Oliver glanced at him as his nerves sizzled. Bane kept his eyes on his plate.

"Charles," Phlox warned. She passed a deep baking dish to Oliver. "So . . ." she began as Oliver scooped layer cake onto his plate. Oliver tried to keep his hand from shaking.

Here it comes, he thought.

"Anything interesting to report from your Saturday?"

Oliver put down the dish and grabbed his fork. "Nah," he said, and started eating. Inside though, he was just waiting.

But one bite, then another, and no one said anything. A minute passed and Oliver finally looked up — to find the rest of them just eating. Oliver wanted to scream, *Do you know or not?*

Finally, Sebastian looked to Oliver, "So, any new dreams lately?" He smiled.

"Um —" The scene from the portal vision ran across his mind. "I think I had another one," Oliver lied, "but I don't remember it."

"Oh, Oliver," Phlox began matter-of-factly, "we were just talking. Your father's Longest Night office party is next Friday. You're welcome to have friends over while we're out, if you want. Maybe you could invite Seth?"

"Maybe," Oliver mumbled.

"He might be excited to get out," continued Phlox. "Francyne and Edward just picked up their new baby. She's such a precious little thing," Phlox said to herself, then added, "but I'm sure their house has been crazy with the new arrival."

Oliver just shrugged. A real vampire child. That must have been nice.

"Or," Phlox tried, "you could invite other friends, if you want."

Oliver almost laughed out loud. Sure! Imagine that: *Actually, Mom, that sounds great! I've got two friends I'd like to have over. You don't mind that they're humans, do you?* Instead, he said, "Okay."

"And then Saturday," Phlox continued, "we're having David and Elanor and your cousins over for Longest Night dinner and gifts."

"Okay," Oliver said again.

There was another moment of silent eating . . . then another . . . and then dinner was over. Bane went out for the evening without a word. Phlox retreated to the kitchen, Sebastian to his study.

Oliver was left sitting there, finishing up and having a hard time believing his luck. Did they really not know what had happened? Well, they might still find out, so he wasn't out of this yet. But with every day that passed, the chances would get smaller that his parents would find out about the Underground. And if he could make it to Friday, then he might just be able to get the file.

❊

Oliver's days seemed more sleepless than ever, yet he almost preferred lying awake, because when he did fall asleep, he was plagued by the vision of his human parents. Incredibly, Sunday passed without any discovery of what had happened in the Underground, which made Oliver breathe easier, but there was still Monday at school to contend with.

He dragged out getting ready, partially because he was so tired. As he and Bane walked up the rainy streets, Oliver kept lagging behind. His backpack felt extra heavy. As they neared the bridge underpass and its troll statue, Bane actually stopped and waited for Oliver to catch up.

Oliver glanced at him, waiting for a taunt. But then Bane said something completely different, "You wanna ditch tonight?"

Oliver was shocked. "Huh?" He tensed inside. It was that strange, brotherly version of Bane again, the one that made Oliver nervous, waiting for the joke.

But as Bane fell into slow step beside him, there didn't seem to be one. "Ty and Randall and I are going to head downtown, see what we can find," Bane explained. "You could come with us."

"I —"

"Come on, bro." He actually slapped Oliver's back as he said this. "We'll work some of that *lamb* out of you."

Oliver didn't know what to say. He couldn't believe that Bane was actually *inviting* him along, yet alarms were going off inside. Could he trust this so-called brother of his? If anything, he wanted to spend as much time as he could this week *not* being around his family. "I . . . I shouldn't," he said finally. "I have a test, I —"

"Bane-o!" A voice shouted from nearby. They had reached the troll. Ty's and Randall's eyes lit up the dark behind it.

"What's up?" Bane called. Then he turned and took Oliver by the shoulder. That was weird, too. And so was what he said next, "You sure?"

Oliver kind of wondered why Bane was giving him the choice. Usually, if Bane wanted Oliver to do something, he just forced him to do it. What was going on with him? And yet, Oliver's old thought about Bane returned. *He knows. He still might not know exactly what's going on, but he definitely knows there's something.* Oliver shrugged. "I . . . I should just go to school."

"Bane! Let's go!" Ty shouted.

Bane looked directly at Oliver, and his eyes looked almost sorry. "All right," he said, sighing. He actually seemed disappointed.

"Is the twerp coming, or what?" Randall called.

Bane gave Oliver a halfhearted shove down the street, then turned to his friends. "The lamb has to run off to school!" he called sarcastically, then disappeared into the shadows.

Oliver continued slowly toward school. The whole way, he thought about ditching on his own. Even as he trudged up the stairs toward class, he still considered turning and getting out of there. But that would only draw more suspicion, and then his teachers might call his parents. Still, his insides knotted as he stepped through the classroom door. *Here it comes,* he thought miserably. Surely, thanks to Theo, everybody knew, and he was going to get it.

There was most of the class, carousing about, on the walls or in groups sitting on desks. Suzyn saw him first, then her friends, and one by one everyone in the room stopped talking and turned toward Oliver. The room slowed to a halt, silent except for Oliver's footsteps across the tile floor. He glanced up, finding Theo, Brent, and Maggots on the wall. They watched him, Theo grinning maliciously. Oliver looked down and rushed to his desk. As he slid into his seat, conversation seeped back into the room.

Oliver looked to Seth beside him. "Hey," he said softly.

Seth was dealing his role-playing cards. He didn't answer.

"Seth," Oliver murmured.

"Don't," Seth whispered out of the corner of his mouth. "Don't do this to me."

"I heard about your new sister —"

But Seth gathered his cards together and slid out of his seat. Oliver sat there, the chaos of the classroom echoing around him, and he couldn't have felt more alone.

❋

As the night went on, snickers bled into the silent treatment, but otherwise, no one talked to him. It stopped bothering Oliver after a couple of hours, and he started feeling defiant about it. What did *they* know anyway?

They were all normal. They couldn't understand what it was like to be him. So, good, fine, whatever. Still, the night took forever to end.

Oliver lagged behind as everyone left, then headed down the first-floor hall to Emalie's classroom. He weaved between the still, perfectly lined desks to Emalie's seat, which wasn't hard for a vampire nose to pick out. He pulled a note from his pocket:

Friday night. Outside my house. 3 AM? –O

He folded it tight and wedged it between the underside of the desktop and one of the metal bars.

●

That morning at dinner was the same. As was Tuesday night at school. Oliver visited Emalie's desk before heading home, to find a return note:

c ya then. –e

He kept the paper.

Wednesday passed normally. It was actually starting to seem like Oliver had gotten extremely lucky. Still, how could it be that every kid at school knew, yet word of the incident at the Underground had not gotten back to his parents? Oliver didn't get it.

Thursday at school was the same as the rest of the

week. Oliver was getting used to being ignored when he bothered to notice. His thoughts were on Friday, on the file. When he got home, Sebastian called to say he would be at work until dawn. Phlox left shortly after dinner for a school board meeting. Bane camped out in the living room, playing videogames online with Ty and Randall.

Oliver had spread out his homework on the kitchen island. But he wasn't doing any of it. What was the point? He couldn't pay attention to anything, at least not until he'd looked at that file. He kept thinking about Friday night, and it occurred to him that since it was incredibly risky to have Emalie and Dean over, he ought to make sure that the file was even in the drawer for them to see. Now, with Bane locked into his game, and his parents out, Oliver slipped out of the kitchen. He passed the living room and dining room, heading down the hall and into the dark study.

There was a wide antique desk that Sebastian had inherited down from the Ming dynasty, with a thin, obsidian glass computer monitor on top. Oliver slid into the leather desk chair, his eyes drawn to the small charcoal sketch of the family beside the monitor. It was from ten years ago. Everyone was gazing with pleasant seriousness, like things couldn't be more normal. Oliver turned away. The file drawer was in the bottom right side of the desk. It had no lock. He reached down to slide it open, but whacked the keyboard tray as he did so. The computer monitor jumped to life in blue light. Oliver froze, listening.

"No way!" he heard Bane shouting at his game, down the hall.

Oliver bent back down and slid open the file drawer. Phlox kept the files well organized. Oliver scanned the titles on the folders. He wasn't sure where it would be, but he saw MEDICAL RECORDS and pulled it out. The file was thin. There were bills for a tooth regeneration here and there, and for the couple of times that Oliver or Bane had broken a limb badly enough to need it splinted overnight, but nothing else.

He slid the file back and kept looking at the folder names. They were normal, mundane things, and if Oliver's information was disguised in one of those, it would take him far too long to find. But then, near the back, he saw a file titled simply NEXIA. Oliver wasn't sure what that word meant, but he felt like he'd heard it somewhere. In school, maybe? The ending -*xia* was sometimes used in the names of higher worlds. He instinctively reached for the folder.

A green force field shimmered into existence for a moment, deflecting his hand. Oliver tried again with the same result. He tried to touch the folder in front of it and could. Same with the one behind it. That had to be the one. There had to be a way to disable the force field somewhere: maybe a spoken password.

Oliver slid the drawer closed. Other than the computer, the desk was empty. He looked through the other drawers, but they were just full of office supplies. Maybe Sebastian had it somewhere on the computer. Oliver pulled out the keyboard. He called up a search window on the screen, then typed in the folder name: NEXIA. The computer began to search.

As it churned, Oliver turned his ear back to the door.

"Got one! Got one!" Bane shouted distantly. "Oh, yeeeaahh!"

Oliver looked back to the screen. The search window flashed: NO RESULTS FOUND. Now what? Well, he still had until tomorrow night to find a way to disable the field. He started to leave the computer when the screen beeped again. A chat box had appeared.

There was a message from MAVincent42: *Seb, are you there? I've taken a look at these photos you sent. I think you're right about him.*

Just turn away, Oliver thought . . . but instead he put his fingers to the keyboard and replied: *I'm here.*

Dr. Vincent replied: *You should bring him back in. Right away. Tell him the FRI results are faulty, and we need to run them again. My mistake.*

Oliver thought about what to say, then typed: *OK. Can you send me the photos? I lost them — computer crashed.*

There was no reply. . . . And then: *Loading them now. . . .*

Oliver watched the chat box as an hourglass spun. Now the corner of a large picture appeared in the tiny box. Oliver dragged the box bigger, until the first photo Dr. Vincent had sent filled the frame.

It took Oliver a moment to believe what he was seeing.

The photo was black and white. It was a view of a room — the abandoned surface level of his house. There was Emalie standing on the floor, in the raincoat she'd worn on her very first visit. And there was the blur of Oliver on the ceiling. Oliver scrolled down. The second picture showed Emalie taking pictures, and a blurry presence hanging down behind her — when he'd tried to take her earring. He scrolled farther. The next picture showed Oliver's blur by the window after they'd left.

The pictures had rounded edges and had been taken from high in the corner of the room. Closed-circuit cameras . . . . Of course, Sebastian would have had security features put in. *You idiot,* Oliver thought, wincing. How could he not have thought of that? Really, though, the only thing that mattered was — *they knew.* His parents knew about Emalie. And they had known since the beginning.

Oliver kept scrolling and was hardly surprised by what he saw now. The next photo showed Oliver's shadowy form leaping off the railing in the Underground, with Emalie and Dean on his back. Who had taken it? Maybe some bystander who smelled a story? Someone his parents had hired? Did it matter?

Another message from Dr. Vincent appeared: *Can you get him in tomorrow after work?*

Oliver typed quickly: *We have plans.*

Dr. Vincent replied: *Seb, I don't think we can afford to wait.*

Oliver was already getting up from the chair as he typed: *All right. After work. Gotta run. Thanks.*

He closed the chat, replaced the chair as it was, then hurried out of the study. Back in the kitchen, he wondered what to do. His brain was spinning. His parents knew everything! And they'd been pretending, lying to him just like he'd been lying to them.

"Take that!" Bane grunted from the other room.

Why hadn't they confronted him? Grounded him like normal parents? *Because what's wrong with you is so serious,* he thought sickly, *they had to wait for the doctor's advice.* There'd be no way to avoid that doctor's appointment tomorrow. Dr. Vincent's office would call to confirm. They always did. And then what?

Something Dr. Vincent had said at the last visit popped back into Oliver's head: *We can always try again.* He'd made it sound like Oliver was an experiment. One that was clearly failing. And what did you do with a failed experiment? You ended it and started over.

"Baaahhh!! Die, humans!" Bane shouted.

Oliver paced around. He had to act like everything was normal, didn't he? At least until the next evening . . . But then what? Go to school? Come home for dinner and act surprised when his parents wanted to take him to the doctor? What other choice did he have? There was no way out of this. Not that Oliver could think of.

But, no. No. He couldn't stay here any longer, thinking, pretending, fearing everything. Grabbing his sweatshirt, he left the kitchen without a sound and headed out into the night. As he slipped out of the sewer at the end of Twilight Lane, Oliver glanced back at his house and had to wonder if he would ever return.

CHAPTER 13

Dress Rehearsal

Oliver headed for Emalie's house. The rain had mixed with sleet, and tiny bits of ice bounced off him as he walked. When he arrived, he saw that the basement was dark but, of course, it was almost four in the morning. There was blue light flickering from the living room. Oliver hopped up on the porch and carefully peered in the window. Emalie's father was asleep on the couch, half-wrapped in a blanket and still in his clothes. Television light washed over him in morphing colors.

Oliver circled around the back of the house and let himself into the basement. He headed up a rickety set of wooden stairs and into the kitchen. He moved silently down the one hallway, past a bathroom, and found another tiny staircase ducking up to the second floor. The stairs ended on a short landing. Up here, the ceilings were low. The top corners of the walls were angled to the slope of the roof. There was a door open to a mess of a bedroom on one end and a closed door at the other.

Oliver quietly opened this door and found himself in Emalie's room.

There were unpacked boxes in the corners, but the walls were covered with a layered patchwork of photographs as if she'd been living here for years. Emalie's bed was beneath the one small window at the far end of the room. He saw her hair above the blankets and could hear her sleeping breaths. He closed the door and moved over to the wall. There was a large box with a laptop on it, and a square pillow pulled up in front of it as a makeshift desk. Oliver sat beside this, pulled his knees up to his elbows, and leaned his head back on the wall.

Outside, the sleet came down harder, rattling the window and tapping drumrolls on the roof. Oliver stared into space, his thoughts unwinding. He found that he actually felt safe. No one from his family could get to him here, without being invited in. *From your fake family,* he thought darkly.

Suddenly, Emalie bolted up in her bed. "What," she whispered. "Don't hurt him. It's not your fault." Her head whipped back and forth, but Oliver could see that her eyes were still closed. "It's —" Now she froze. Oliver watched as she turned toward him, and her eyes slowly opened. She squinted, then rubbed at her long tangles of hair. Oliver wondered if he should spectralize, but then Emalie spoke:

"Hey," she said groggily.

"Hey," Oliver replied.

"What are you doing here?"

"I didn't know where to go," Oliver said truthfully. "My parents know about you. They know about everything."

Emalie put her feet on the floor and scratched at her head. Then she got up, crossing the room to an open box beside the closet. She rummaged around, then pulled out a blanket. She threw it to him as she headed back to bed. "What are you going to do?" she asked, sliding back under her blankets.

"I don't know," Oliver muttered.

"Well, you should stay here," Emalie said. "I have school tomorrow, and after that Dean and I have a dress rehearsal for our holiday concert. You can hang out here during the day."

"What about your dad?"

"He'll be out for most of the day, probably," Emalie said. "But you're pretty good at not being seen."

Oliver pulled the blanket over him. It felt scratchy compared to the dirt in his coffin, but it warmed him almost as well. The sound of the sleet seemed very loud to him. You could barely hear such a thing from a crypt. A car rushed by outside, and a warped rectangle of light crossed the room. Now Oliver noticed stars on the ceiling. They seemed to be glowing stickers, and they were arranged in perfect constellations. He saw Scorpio, Orion, Cassiopeia.

Oliver looked over at Emalie. She was looking back at him. "How come you're not scared of me?" he asked.

Emalie shrugged. "I don't know. You don't seem that scary."

Oliver smiled. That was almost an insult for a vampire, but he didn't mind.

"Well," Emalie went on, propping herself up with her elbow on her pillow, "I mean, you're kinda scary. I don't know, I think the only people that scare me are the ones who like themselves too much, and who think they're always right. You don't seem to like yourself too much."

"But I'm not *people*," said Oliver. "I'm not even a person."

"I think you're a person," said Emalie. "And . . . I mean, you were one. You were born a human just like the rest of us."

Oliver looked around the room, trying to imagine being a human kid. Waking up and looking in a mirror, then out a window to decide what to wear. After a minute, he looked back at Emalie, expecting her to be asleep, but she wasn't. "What happened to your mom?" Oliver asked.

There was a moment of silence, and Oliver wondered if he shouldn't have asked. But then Emalie sighed and said, "Nobody knows. She's been gone for two years. She was a flight attendant. She left one morning like any other day. And that was it." She glanced out the window. "My dad is still sad. He keeps trying to look for her, but he doesn't know how."

"Sorry," Oliver said.

Emalie kept gazing out at the sleet. Headlights slid across her face. When she continued, Oliver thought she might sound sad, but she didn't. "I see her sometimes, in my dreams. She's always somewhere ancient. I don't know why. I mean, she liked history and visiting old places. Maybe that's what makes me think of it. Whenever I dream about her, it's like I'm in her head, looking out through her eyes. Like I am her, or something. It's messed up."

"Maybe you really are," Oliver said, thinking about what Désirée had told him. She'd referred to Emalie as an Orani — a seer. The Orani were an ancient and secretive order of humans, known for their ability to "see" into a person's future. The Orani were also rumored to be able to read people's minds, even communicate with wraiths and spirits in the other worlds. Oliver remembered hearing that where most humans had only a tiny bit of intuition, the Orani could use intuition like a whole other sixth sense. They could sense one's attitudes, desires, and fears, and guess what they would do in the future, with startling accuracy. These powers had actually caused the Orani lots of trouble in history. They had been regularly imprisoned and kept as slaves by kings and leaders, and sometimes burned at the stake by fearful villagers. Some governments had done awful experiments on them, such that the Orani kept their identity secret. Emalie didn't even seem to know that she was one, yet, but the fact that she joined Oliver in the portal vision made it likely that she really was.

An Orani's sight was passed down the generations. To Oliver, it didn't sound strange at all for Emalie to be sharing visions with her mother. Oliver tried to think of a way to explain this to Emalie, but she was moving on —

"Yeah, right," she said, rolling over. "She's probably dead, or happy. Either way, she's gone."

Oliver couldn't think of anything else to say. If he found a way out of his current mess, he'd have to help Emalie learn more about her identity.

The sleet was changing back to rain. Water ran down the window in sheets. "Good night, Emalie," Oliver whispered.

"Gnnd," Emalie mumbled. Soon her sleeping breaths returned and, as he would find to his surprise later on, Oliver fell asleep as well.

He awoke in the early afternoon to dull orange light. He was lying on his side, curled up on the floor, and Emalie had thrown her thick orange comforter over the rest of him. She'd also thought to hang a blanket over the bare window.

Oliver found the house empty. He also found that he was starving. He went to the kitchen. There was little that a vampire would like, but he did find a sugary cereal: Count Chocula. He frowned but poured a bowl and turned to sit, only the kitchen table was bathed in daylight. He went into the living room but found the same problem with the couch. He ended up eating in the bathroom.

After that, he felt better, but was still thirsty, so he headed into the basement to find a rat or at least a mouse. Then he returned upstairs. He looked around for a while but didn't know what to do with himself. Returning to Emalie's room, he tried going back to sleep, but it didn't work. His thoughts were only getting more crazy as the afternoon went on. By now, Phlox and Sebastian would definitely be looking for him in the Underground. They might even have figured out what *he* knew about what *they* knew. Oliver wished more than anything that there was some way to just make this entire situation go away, but how? There didn't seem to be a solution.

At four in the afternoon, Oliver headed for school. It was the evening before Longest Night, and so darkness had already started to fall on the city. For the humans, this was the last day of school before their Christmas vacation. There was an excited speed to the way everyone was moving. It was cold, the wind whipping a light rain so that it felt like pinpricks. Oliver leaped onto the back of a passing bus and rode it until he was near school.

Rodrigo hadn't even arrived yet. Oliver let himself in. The halls were quiet. The cheery holiday decorations had yet to be overrun by grotesqua. Oliver crept up to the main floor. He heard light talking and shuffling of papers in the main office. Then the faint sound of singing voices reached his ears. Oliver headed toward it.

At the end of the hall he reached a set of double doors. He peered inside. The lights were off except for spotlights. They were aimed at two sets of risers on the floor in front of the stage. The chorus stood there, their teacher in front. Behind them, the curtain was pulled closed across the stage and decorated with the cut-out snowflakes from the art room. Behind the conductor, empty chairs were arranged in neat rows. The kids were in the middle of a bouncy song about winter.

Oliver slid inside. He concentrated, spectralizing, then scaled the wall. He reached the high ceiling, crossed it, and stopped at the metal scaffolding that hung down and held a basketball hoop. He slid down one of these poles and sat on top of the backboard.

Emalie was in the second row. She was wearing a hooded brown sweater, and surprisingly, had her hair down. Dean was in the back. Everyone else was staring at the teacher as they sang, but Emalie looked around now and then. Oliver wondered if she was looking for him.

As with the human children's art, this chorus wasn't very skilled by vampire standards. Still, listening to these middle-school voices was nice, despite their flaws. Oliver enjoyed how their singing echoed around the giant box of a room. He also enjoyed the hollow silences between songs, when the resonance of the last song still lingered, and the anticipation for the next song was building. They sang for another half hour, during which time Oliver relaxed and barely thought about his troubles. Finally, the last piece ended and the students began to gather their things.

"Remember," their teacher was saying, "everyone must be here by six tomorrow night to warm up before the show. Don't forget to —" Her voice was cut off by a loud banging, from a door down in the hallway beside the stage. The teacher huffed and headed toward the hall. "I've asked you before, students," she grumbled, "to please tell your parents to wait outside until I excuse you."

She disappeared into the hall, and Oliver looked back to Emalie. She was looking right at him and waved quickly. The other students were beginning to head out the double doors into the hall.

Oliver heard the back door opening and the teacher saying, "I'm sorry, but the school is closed and we're in the middle of —" but then her voice cut off. There was a loud thud. A couple of students heard it and turned.

"All right, everyone!" A high-pitched voice called. It sounded like a girl — no, like a boy pretending to be a girl —

Bane and his friends stormed into the gym. Oliver froze. Some of the students looked up. They had no reason to suspect what was really happening.

Bane was carrying a long staff. He leaned it against his shoulder and clapped his hands together, continuing in his fake teacher's voice, "Places, please! Let's get these songs into shape!"

The humans, at least, recognized that Bane and his friends were bullies, and they scowled and hurried their steps toward the door. Oliver saw Dean grab Emalie's arm to leave, but she was staring hard at Bane.

"Chop-chop!" Bane yelled in the girl's voice. And then he shoved the nearest human, a boy, and sent him flying across the room.

Now the kids started to run for the door.

"Randall!" Bane barked in his normal voice.

Randall sprinted past him and leaped into the air, flying across the room and landing just in front of the double doors. He turned and crossed his arms.

Someone screamed.

"Nobody leaves!" Bane shouted. "Not until we straighten a few things out."

Oliver slipped back up the pole to the ceiling. Now he counted: There were twelve kids left in the gym. They all backed away from Bane and Ty at one end, and Randall at the other, until they formed a tight group in front of the risers. Ty and Bane separated, forming a triangle around the group.

"Hey, kids," Bane said, lowering his voice and flashing a devilish grin that revealed the points of his teeth. "No need to worry. This won't take long, and it may not even hurt that bad." As he said this, he waved the staff in the kids' directions. Oliver had never seen it before. The humans were silent. Now one of them whimpered. Bane turned his head. "Hey, little brother!" he shouted into the dark recesses of the gym.

Oliver pressed against the ceiling, but he already knew it was no use.

"Come on, little lamb, you *know* I know you're here."

Oliver tried to think of what to do, but his thoughts were a blur.

"Look," Bane called. "Big brother is here to help, so if you don't come down, here's what I'm going to do: I'm going to kill each of these kids, one at a time, until you do — starting with this one!"

Bane lunged and grabbed a shorter girl from the edge of the group. She screamed as he pulled her near, dropping her music folder, its sheets spilling across the floor.

"All right!" Oliver vaulted off the ceiling, landing beside Bane. He glared at his so-called brother with all the hate he could muster.

Bane just smiled. "Hey, kid," he said, and shoved the girl back into the terrified group. "You know you've got Mom and Dad worried sick."

Oliver shook his head. "Yeah, right," he muttered. "Just get out of here, Bane."

"Ha, whatever. I knew we'd find you here. It was so *obvious*." Bane turned toward the kids. "So . . . which ones are they?"

Oliver didn't risk even glancing at the humans. "They're not here —"

Bane rolled his eyes. "Duh! Of *course,* they're here. That's why you're here. So, come on, point out your *cow* friends. Don't make me guess."

"Bane!" Oliver snapped. "Come on, you found me. Just take me home, and you can be the big hero."

Bane looked at Oliver for a long moment. Oliver found, right then, that he just had no idea what was going through Bane's mind. Finally, Bane sighed. "Nah. You need help, bro. That's why I'm here. If I take you home, it's going to be all with the *what's wrong with our baby?!* And I am just — sick — of that." Bane threw an arm around Oliver's shoulder. "Nope, we're going to fix you, right here, right now."

Oliver shoved Bane away. "I'm fine. Just leave me alone!"

"Believe me, I'd *love* to! But you're my best excuse for a brother," Bane said, and threw his arm around Oliver again, this time, with a grip that Oliver couldn't break. "That's why Bane's here to make it all better." As he said this, Bane pointed at the humans with the staff he was carrying. It was made of basic wood, except for the top, where a bony hand of metal held a crystal sphere. Turquoise light swirled inside the sphere. Oliver had never seen it before and didn't know what it might be, yet it looked like something enchanted.

Now Bane twisted Oliver toward the crowd of terrified human faces, then spoke softly by Oliver's ear, but still loud enough for everyone in the room to hear, "Now, pick one."

"What?"

"You heard me. Pick the lucky human who's going to be your first victim."

The humans gasped and cried out.

"Everybody shut up, please," Ty said gleefully.

"No! Bane." Oliver struggled against his grip. "I'm not. I won't."

"You are, little brother," Bane snarled, "And you will. Sometimes you gotta grow up early, and that's what you're going to do right now. So pick one, or I'll pick *for* you."

Oliver's eyes darted from one child to the next, trying with all his might *not* to linger on Emalie or Dean. What could he do? He was trying to think —

"Three seconds, little bro," Bane announced, his grip on Oliver's shoulder tightening. "One . . ."

Oliver squirmed, but it was no use. He looked miserably across the terrified faces, and as he passed Emalie, he saw her mouth moving. Oliver watched her in the corner of his eye. What was she saying? It looked like, *Pick me.*

No. He couldn't. She probably felt responsible, like this was all her fault.

"Two . . ." Bane called dramatically.

Oliver looked desperately around. He couldn't do this, he —

"Three!" Bane announced. He flashed a triumphant

look at Oliver, then turned and pointed right at Emalie. "I choose her!"

"No!" Oliver screamed.

"Um, yeah. Ty!"

Ty moved toward the group, grinning at Emalie.

"All right, fine!" shouted Oliver, trying to shake free. "I'll choose!"

Bane finally let him go. "Do it now, lamb," he hissed.

Oliver glanced at the group. A plan was finally forming in his head. It didn't feel very possible, but he would at least need someone to play along. So Oliver leaped forward, shooting into the crowd and slamming into Dean. He grabbed Dean's shoulders, and the two hit the floor and slid toward the wall.

"Oliver, no! Don't!" Dean stammered as they came to a halt. "Please!"

"Relax!" Oliver hissed into his ear. "I'm not going to, I just — I had to do something. Now scream —" Dean didn't do anything. "Scream!" Oliver snapped, and moved his head closer to Dean's neck trying to make it look like he was biting Dean.

"Ahhh — noo!" Dean screamed. Oliver kept his face by Dean's neck but glanced up toward the double doors. Randall was watching them with a wide smile on his face. Maybe he was distracted enough that Oliver could surprise him. Oliver readied to jump. Dean was still putting on a good show of screaming, though Oliver could tell that he really was terrified. And Oliver thought sadly that Dean was right to be scared: Because even though Oliver told himself he would *never* bite Dean, with his face right by Dean's neck like this, his vampire senses could feel Dean's pulse. He could hear the blood racing through Dean's arteries. A wave of hopelessness flashed over Oliver. How could he fight what he was? *No,* he thought. *That's not what I am!*

"Come on, Oliver!" Bane shouted from behind. Oliver tensed, preparing to jump free of Dean —

But suddenly, there was an explosion of sparkling turquoise light. Oliver was blinded. *Bane,* he just had time to start thinking . . .

When a strange voice thundered in his head, so loud that it drowned out all his thoughts, *Oliver, don't fight it, my boy. It's time.*

Oliver lost all feeling in his body, lost track of his senses, his surroundings, and time.

CHAPTER 14

The Gate and the Stake

The turquoise light was replaced by darkness. Oliver had a sense of rising, of leaving his body and reality behind and moving through worlds. Was this another portal? It seemed to be.

Barriers of energy fluttered aside like curtains. Oliver couldn't see himself, but he had a sense that he was floating, moving through dark space at an incredible speed. Around him there were shrouded forms, like clouds at night. And occasionally, white streaks of light in the distance.

Suddenly, there was land below. Oliver saw a rocky landscape of knife-edge mountains and canyons of glowing lava. He wondered if this was a level of the Underworld, yet there were brilliant stars above, more brilliant than he'd ever seen, along with planets, and brushstrokes of galaxies that seemed close enough to touch.

And he was moving faster and faster. Now he saw buildings down among the mountains and canyons, buildings that glowed as if made of fabulous minerals — yet they blurred beneath him. More galaxies above, and nebulae of brilliant colors, like smudged rainbows, littered with diamonds. Yet they were a blur, too.

Oliver. The voice spoke again. It was calm, serene, and ancient. *This is the first step into a higher world for you.*

Who are you? Oliver thought back wildly.

I am Illisius. I am your demon.

Illisius, Oliver repeated, feeling like, in some way, he'd known the name forever.

Welcome.

Where am I? Oliver asked.

You are in Nexia, where all worlds meet, the birthplace of the forces, where you will soon travel.

I don't —

You don't need to know. Illisius's voice was all around him, soothing. *All you need to know is that when you are ready, you will journey here. Then we will open the Gate, and free the vampyr from Earth.*

Me? How?

In time, I will show you. You have already taken the first steps.

But, I'm not —

Oliver . . . This is your destiny. You are the only one who can do this. And you must. Let no one tell you otherwise.

How —

I will visit you again soon. Until then, all you need to know is ahead of you now.

Oliver looked ahead. He was weaving through a maze of canyons, their red walls rising precipitously all around him. Now something incredibly bright shone in the far distance. Its light was golden, and silver, and rose, and pure white.

Oliver burst free of the canyon. Vast plains of red rock spread into the distance. He saw a single black road snaking along beneath him. To either side, the horizon seemed infinitely far, yet in the sky, planets hung so close he felt like he could grab them.

But that light ahead — it was amazing — and even though it nearly blinded him to look at it, that was all he wanted to do. Just stare into it, and he did.

Vaguely, he noticed a man standing far below on the road as he raced overhead, toward the light with its indescribable color . . . and more than that . . . this light felt alive. He almost felt like he *knew* it . . . like if he just stared long enough, he could see the face of it, of the Gate —

Oliver, the Gate said in his mind. Its voice seemed familiar, too. *See me clearly.* Oliver squinted, trying, and almost thought he could make out a shape in the overwhelming light —

Then he was past it. He tried to crane his neck to look behind him, but he was moving too quickly. The red land was disappearing below him. Space was returning . . . worlds pushing aside again, rushing faster. Still, that light burned in Oliver's eyes, a leftover brightness that he didn't want to lose.

✻

The light lingered. Slowly, Oliver felt himself returning to reality. As he did, part of an ancient lullaby ran through his mind . . .

See the sun or the stake you must,
Run right home or turn to dust.

His mother, Phlox — *not your mother!* he thought suddenly — used to sing that to him as she tucked him in at night. Oliver felt a deep ache. Phlox had a beautiful alto's voice, having trained for fifty years in Vienna. She would sing and smooth Oliver's soil just so, and what was that memory now? Was it real, or a lie? It seemed so simple, and maybe that was why he'd thought of it. Things weren't simple anymore — maybe they never would be again.

Oliver felt his arms and legs, and now something hard against his back. Floor. He blinked hard, and the brightness faded and started to separate, into squares, with dark lines.

It was a tall window. The light coming through it was not that wonderful light from the Gate. It was the soft orange of streetlights. Oliver sat up to find himself in his classroom, upstairs. He was sitting between the rows of desks. He rubbed at his head, then at his jaw. Everything felt sore.

What had happened? The last thing he remembered was pretending to attack Dean and getting ready to jump at Randall. Had he? He wasn't sure, because then there was that weird flash of turquoise, and then the red world, Nexia, the voice of Illisius, and the brilliant Gate.

Something creaked behind him. Oliver cocked his head and heard footsteps slowly entering the room. He turned, but he knew it was Emalie. She was moving behind him, her back against the wall, passing in and out of the distorted rectangles of streetlight. The sleeve of her sweater was torn, and her hair was a mess around her face. She glanced at him, and Oliver saw her red-rimmed eyes and tear-streaked face, before she looked away.

"Emalie," Oliver began.

She stopped and slid down the wall, sitting and hugging her knees. She started to cry quietly.

Oliver felt a sinking feeling inside, but he wasn't sure

why. Something was very wrong, though. "What happened?" he asked. She didn't answer. "What am I doing up here?" He twisted around and started to get to his feet.

"Stop." Emalie looked up, and her gaze was awful. She held out her arms, shaking. Clutched in both hands was her wooden stake.

Oliver froze, staring at the stake. Why did she have that with her at school? And how many other times had she had it along that Oliver hadn't known about? "What are you doing with that thing?"

"Stop it," Emalie said darkly. "Stop talking like a human. Stop looking at me like a human. You're *not* human."

The sinking feeling inside Oliver was getting worse. "What happened? I don't —"

But Emalie's face crumbled and she started to cry, silently, again.

Oliver stood up. He listened, but the school was silent. Where were Bane and his friends? The other students?

Now a faint sound reached his ears from outside, a wailing, growing louder. It was a siren. Oliver turned back to Emalie, as something occurred to him.

"Emalie," he said quietly, barely daring to ask, "Where's Dean?"

Emalie's face twisted further, and she sobbed.

"Oh, no," he mumbled aloud. Oliver started to shake, squeezing his fists so tightly that his nails dug into his palms. "Bane . . . Emalie, I'm sorry, he . . ."

"NO!" she shouted at him, pushing back up the wall and waving the stake at him. "You aren't sorry! Monsters can't be sorry!"

"N . . . no," Oliver stammered. "I know, but Bane and I are different. I would never hurt anyone. He —"

"Ha!" Emalie spat. "Stop it!" she yelled.

"Stop what?" Oliver asked desperately.

"You killed Dean!" Emalie screamed, waving the stake at him. "You killed Dean!"

Oliver was stunned. "I — Wait . . . No, I didn't! I —"

"Stop trying to lie, Oliver! I saw you do it!"

"What?!" Oliver felt like the world was spinning around him. He was beginning to wonder if this was still a dream, or maybe another portal. He hoped it was, and yet the awful swirling pit that was forming in his stomach knew better. This was real, terribly real.

"You jumped on him, and he screamed," Emalie sobbed. "And you bit him in the neck and you just kept biting and he was shouting for help and I couldn't get to him, I —" Emalie shuddered, twisting at the hole in her sweater. "And then he stopped shouting. He stopped moving . . . and you jumped up and ran out of the room!" Emalie swallowed a sob. "Then your friends let us go. But I didn't leave. I couldn't."

There were more sirens now. They were getting louder, closer. Oliver could hear voices outside. People were coming. What was Emalie talking about? How could he have done such a thing? There was no way —

"Emalie," he said desperately, "I don't remember anything after I jumped. But I couldn't have! I was going to try to get us out of there. It must have been Bane, he probably —"

"Look at you!" she shouted.

"What?"

"Look at your face!" Emalie shook her head. "Oh, that's right, you can't. Because you're a monster!"

Oliver reached to his face with shaking fingers. He touched his cheek, by his mouth, and came away with flakes of — blood.

No. No! How could he have done it? Why didn't he remember? "Emalie, I didn't . . . I wasn't even there! I had this vision, but still — I . . . I couldn't —" Without thinking, he took a step toward her.

"Stop! If you come closer I'll stake you, Oliver, I swear." Her hands shook, the stake wavering back and forth.

The sirens were joined by roaring engines circling into the parking lot. Shoes slapped on stairs, and now the doors to the school were bursting open.

"In here!" a woman's voice — the choral teacher — shouted.

Emalie started sliding back toward the door.

"Emalie, please," Oliver begged. "You have to believe me —"

"How could you?" She started to cry again. "How could you, Oliver?" Then she dropped the stake and ran out.

Oliver watched the stake rolling on the floor. *Maybe you should pick it up, maybe you should just —*

But now he heard boots thundering up the stairs. "She said he's up here!"

Oliver bolted for the door, then turned and staggered down the hall. He could distantly hear more commotion downstairs: parents, students, paramedics. He wanted so badly, *needed* to get back down there. How could he have killed Dean? There was no way. It was just impossible. There had to be another explanation — but what? An enchantment of some kind? A trick? Yet he couldn't help hearing Emalie's voice: *How could you?* And now he'd lost her forever.

He reached a janitor's closet and slid inside, then spun to peer out the cracked door. Two police officers rushed across the hallway into the classroom where he'd just been. Oliver heard more crying downstairs.

He stood frozen for a moment, not knowing what else to do, but then the officers emerged and started moving up the hall toward him. They split up to check the next two classrooms. Oliver ducked back into the closet, squeezing between two supply shelves. On the back wall was a small metal door: a trash chute. Oliver pulled it open and slid inside. He dropped down into darkness, all the way to the basement. From there, he escaped into the sewers, through the secret door that the vampires used in the bright months of the year.

Eventually, he stopped in an abandoned side tunnel and just sat, for how many hours he didn't know. He couldn't believe what he'd done. And yet, he felt *sure* that he hadn't killed Dean, despite what Emalie had said. It just wasn't possible. *But you're a vampire,* he reminded himself bitterly. A monster, as Emalie had put it. So wasn't it possible? Maybe that vision, from Illisius, had put him in some kind of trance. No, there had to be something else. Bane had that staff. There was that blue light. What had Bane done? *Or did he do anything?* Hours went by. Oliver just sat, not knowing what to do to next. Where could he even go? Yet there was really only one place left for him, and so he got up and trudged off.

CHAPTER 15

Longest Night

Oliver closed the door and paused at the base of the stairs. He listened: The house was silent. Still, he walked as quietly as he could down the hall to the bathroom. He hunched over the wide stone sink in the center of the room and cleaned his face. Then he headed upstairs. The kitchen was still. Everyone was probably out looking for him. What to do now? But Oliver knew his plan, there was no point second-guessing it. He was going to sit down in the living room, play some videogames, and wait. His parents would return, and whatever was going to happen would happen. Whatever punishment he received was going to be nothing compared to the way he felt inside. He was a vampire who needed to be fixed. *And one with a destiny*, he reminded himself. But the thought didn't cheer him up at all. Oliver grabbed a soda from the refrigerator and walked into the dark living room. He headed straight toward the TV.

Suddenly, the lights flicked on.

"SURPRISE!" Oliver whipped around to find Phlox, Sebastian, his aunt Elanor and uncle David, his cousins Nina and Emmett, and even Bane, all sitting around the living room, looking at him —

And smiling. Oliver had no idea what to think.

"Well, Oliver," Sebastian said, standing and clapping him on the back. "Charles told us everything. We were pretty worried before, but, well, now I guess congratulations are in order, aren't they?"

"We're so relieved!" Phlox said, joining them and giving Oliver a big hug. She whispered in his ear, "We just wish you'd let us in on your big secret."

"What?" Oliver asked blankly.

Sebastian smiled again, and Oliver thought he looked more relaxed, more relieved than he'd looked in a long time. "We didn't know what to think when you started befriending those humans, but then Charles explained that it was all part of your clever plan to get them to trust you, so that you could take your first human bite."

"He's a prodigy!" Uncle David called from the couch.

"In front of a crowd, no less," gushed Aunt Elanor, "and the cousin of the girl! That's practically diabolical!"

Oliver wanted to run from the room.

"I'm just glad I was there to see it, bro," Bane added, slouched comfortably in a chair. Oliver turned, and Bane offered him a sly wink, as if they'd been coconspirators.

Oliver wanted to throw out his hands and scream, *Stop!* He wanted to explain what had really happened — but now he was being led to an open chair beside the family's Longest Night tree. One of the tiny, leathery lizards nestled in its silver cage ornament hissed approvingly at him.

"I am just glad this is all behind us," said Phlox, glancing at Oliver. He thought he caught a warning in her voice, but she turned to the rest of the family with a smile.

And just like that, the Nocturnes' celebration of the Longest Night went on, as if everything was normal. Oliver just sat there, numb, watching everyone: his family. He didn't really believe that his parents actually thought everything was all right, with all they'd kept from him before. But he could tell that they were trying really hard. Which meant that, once again, Oliver was alone with his problems. So he opened gifts when they did, and smiled at Uncle David's stories, and all the while felt like he was watching someone else's world from inside his head.

He understood now that he had Bane to thank for this. Bane had, in his own twisted way, saved Oliver, as far as his parents and the vampire world were concerned. By setting him up to kill Dean, he'd created an excuse for all of Oliver's weird behavior over the last few months, one that allowed Phlox and Sebastian, and probably Dr. Vincent and everyone else, to feel like they understood what Oliver had been up to, and to actually be proud of him. It was a pretty amazing feat, and yet, Oliver felt no gratitude for it.

"Aren't you going to thank me?" Bane said later that night, when they ran into each other alone in the kitchen.

Oliver glared at him.

"Not that I expected all *this*," Bane went on sulkily, filling his goblet. "*I* didn't get a surprise party for my first kill."

"How did you do it?" Oliver hissed.

Bane looked up and smiled again. "Me?" he said like he was shocked. "All I did was put you in the right place. Then it was *you*, bro. All you."

"What about that staff? Was it enchanted? What did you —"

Bane's smile faded. "Hey, listen: You're the big hero now." He reached over and patted Oliver on the back, only a little too hard. "So don't screw it up, already." Bane scowled and walked out.

Oliver wanted to shout after him: *I didn't kill Dean!* He wanted to shout it loud enough for the whole party to hear. He still felt sure that he hadn't, and yet, as far as his family was concerned, not only had he killed Dean, but that was something to be celebrated. *Celebrated by your vampire family,* he thought, and was reminded once again of his human parents. Yet thinking of them was like thinking of Emalie: What good did it do? They were gone. He wasn't human like them. He was a vampire, whether he liked it or not. And yet, his brain was still sifting through ideas of how to prove to Emalie that he hadn't killed Dean, how to get her back, and how to find out more about his human parents. For now, though, there was nothing else to be done but to smile and play along with the festivities.

Soon, everyone moved to the living room for a feast. After that, Oliver played videogames with his cousins and may have forgotten about Emalie and Dean for a second or two while he did so.

But much later that morning, when he finally crawled into his coffin for the first time in days, they stormed back into his thoughts, and he missed them terribly, and there was certainly no getting to sleep.

✸

Three days later was the human festival of Christmas. A day before that, a collection of humans, dressed all in black, gathered on a drizzling morning beneath leafless trees, to bury a loved one that they had lost. Human lives were short, sometimes far too short. A vampire, who considered lives in centuries, could never understand how it might feel to have a life pass so quickly. And even when one of their kind turned to dust too soon, a vampire had no idea of how a heart could ache. It just wasn't possible. Yet in the shadow of a moldy mausoleum just up the hill from this funeral scene, beneath a dark grove of pine trees, there was one vampire, watching in secret, who wanted more than anything to understand.

When the ceremony was over, Oliver watched the line of mourners heading to their cars. He watched Emalie, her head down, and yet wearing a bright knit hat against the chilling rain, a splotch of color that made her seem like the only thing in color, in a drab gray world. Maybe Oliver couldn't understand how short a human life could be, but he found that he could understand very well how long his existence was going to be without his friend.

✹

Oliver returned home that evening, his parents thinking he'd spent the day sleeping over at Seth's. Lies like that were already easier, beneath this new glow of vampire pride that surrounded him: Oliver, the devious prodigy child. Nobody wanted to talk about those anxious weeks when Oliver had been acting strangely. Nobody even asked if he'd been sleeping better. Maybe they assumed he was. But he wasn't. Really, for Oliver, it was like he was right back where he started, only worse.

He shuffled through the kitchen, past Phlox. "Hi, Oliver."

Oliver was lost in thought and forgot to reply.

"Hey," Phlox said.

"Yeah?" Oliver's back was still to her.

"Oh," Phlox said. "I was just wondering how your sleepover was."

Oliver nodded, still facing away. "It was fine."

"And everything's all right?" she asked. "You look a little down."

"I'm fine." He almost started walking, then remembered to add, "Mom."

"I like Seth," said Phlox. "He seems like a good friend. Maybe you'd like to have him over for your birthday party this weekend?"

Oliver shrugged. He'd actually forgotten all about his birthday. And now that he remembered it, he realized that it had new meaning. His birthday was the day he was born to Phlox and Sebastian, but it was also the day that he and his human parents had died. It made sense to him now that this was why he'd always been anxious at this time of year. Some part of him had always felt the echo of that awful night. "All right," he said blankly, and started to leave the room.

"Honey . . ." Oliver looked back to find Phlox gazing at him lovingly. "You're probably still feeling a little weird after the other night."

Oliver shrugged. "Guess."

"Well, don't worry. The first bite can be hard, but you'll feel better than ever as time goes by."

"Okay." Oliver turned again.

"You're growing up fast," Phlox added, her voice getting scratchy.

"Mmm."

"Just remember, if you ever want to talk about anything, we're here, okay?"

"All right," Oliver mumbled.

"Because no matter what," added Phlox, "we love you."

"I love you, too, Mom," Oliver answered, and as he left the room, he wondered if he'd been referring to someone else entirely.

✶

School went on break for a week for the Longest Night holiday. When Oliver walked in on the first day back, he didn't know what to expect.

"There he is!" A voice shouted when he was not

two steps into the room. With a rush of air, Theo landed in front of him. He stood tall in front of Oliver, but strangely, Brent and Maggots stayed on the wall.

"What?" Oliver muttered. Out of the corner of his eye, he noticed Suzyn and the other girls looking their way. Once again, with Oliver's arrival, conversation in the classroom had slowed to a halt.

Theo's arms shot forward, shoving Oliver — but only lightly. "Why didn't you tell us, you freak?"

Oliver shrugged weakly. "What are you talking about?"

"With the humans," Theo went on, "why didn't you let us in on it?"

"Oh." Oliver nodded. He'd gotten used to the way things had changed at home, but he hadn't expected it here as well. Everyone in his family was treating him like he was someone to be proud of. It wasn't just that they thought his problems were over. They seemed to look at him differently, like he was special — almost like he'd become some kind of celebrity.

And now, as he finally looked up, Oliver saw it in Theo's eyes, too. The contempt was gone. Theo almost looked, afraid? That wasn't possible, and yet that's what Oliver sensed from him right now. So Oliver threw back his shoulders. "Well, why would I tell you guys? You might have given it away."

Theo smirked, but again, there was some uncertainty to it. "Well, it's a good thing we were there in the Underground, huh? We really helped you out by exposing the humans, so you could make your big escape, the one everyone in town is talking about."

Oliver shrugged. The idea that everyone in town was talking about it was news to him, but he played along. "Sure."

Theo kept smiling, but now he raised his voice so everyone could clearly hear. "So I guess we were a pretty important part of your plan, then?"

Oliver almost laughed out loud. And he realized that his chance to get Theo back for so many moments of torment had arrived. Everyone in class was listening, and, unbelievably, Oliver had the power. He could crush Theo right here, right now. But instead, he said, "Thanks," flatly, and slid past Theo.

He felt eyes on him as he slid into his desk, and heard Theo jump back up to the wall. "I knew it," he said to Brent and Maggots, but loudly enough for the girls to hear: "If it hadn't been for us, he wouldn't be the big story he is."

Oliver slumped in his seat.

"Hey, Oliver," Seth said, looking up from his cards.

"Hey."

"Thanks again for having me at your party," he said a little too eagerly.

While Oliver had to admit that life was easier living with this newest lie, the one where he was a vampire to be respected and maybe even feared, one who had displayed treachery that had even fooled his own family, in order to make his first human bite —

It did nothing for Oliver on the inside. It was like he'd been handed a cruel joke of a consolation prize for losing what mattered to him most. *You aren't sorry!* Emalie's words echoed in his mind. *Monsters can't be sorry!*

Yet he was. Not that she would believe him. Not until he found a way to prove to her that he hadn't killed Dean.

Mr. VanWick swept in, and the night's lessons began. Oliver leaned on his desk, half-listening as they finished the chapter on the Aztecs and moved on to the cannibal tribes of the South Pacific. Eventually, he slid back in his seat.

His knee brushed something underneath his desk. It crinkled like paper. Oliver sat up. Looking around to make sure no one had heard, he slipped his hand along the underside of his desk. There, wedged between the desktop and the metal legs, Oliver found a tightly folded paper. He removed it, opening it slowly beneath the desk. Then, as Mr. VanWick turned toward the blackboard, he slid it onto his textbook.

It was a photocopy of a newspaper article. The headline read:

CHRISTMAS TRAGEDY:
Mother and Father Slain, Child Missing

There was a grainy black-and-white photo beneath
the headline, of police officers milling around the
Christmas tree — the one Oliver remembered from
the portal vision. He glanced at the date above the headline: sixty-three years ago. The article began beneath
the photo:

> SEATTLE — DEC. 29 — A young fam-
> ily was attacked in cold blood last
> night. The mother and father, Mr.
> Howard Bailey and wife, Lindsey, were
> found dead beneath the city Christmas
> tree. The whereabouts of their infant
> son, Nathan, remain unknown, but
> police have issued an all points bulle-
> tin. *(Continued on p. A4)*

Oliver quickly folded the paper and shoved it into his
pocket. His anxiety had returned in a rush. He knew
their names, and his own.

But Oliver also knew, from the scent of the paper, that Emalie knew as well. She had researched the portal vision, left this message for him — which meant there was still a chance that he'd see her again. Still a chance that she could help him find out more about who he was, and who he was meant to be.

About the Author

Kevin Emerson is not currently a vampire, but he does live in Seattle, where it is often gloomy. He also stalks about town after dark, playing drums and singing in bands. For five years, Kevin had to get up too early to teach elementary school science in Boston. After that, he taught writing for three years, but only in the afternoons. Now, he works at a writing center called 826 Seattle.

Kevin has been writing stories since he was a kid. One time, he ran out of ideas and became worried that his creativity had left him forever, much like a hubcap escaping the wheel of a car that is careening down a twisting highway along the edge of a cliff by the sea. It turns out he was just hungry and tired. After a nice omelet and yet another cup of coffee, everything was fine.

Stop by and say hello at: www.kevinemerson.net

OLIVER'S ADVENTURES CONTINUE...

TURN THE PAGE FOR A SNEAK PREVIEW.

The crime scene photos were grim. A boy, lying in a school gymnasium, blood around his neck . . .

"I suppose they're calling it a stabbing or something," said Detective Nick Pederson, leaning over his desk.

"The boys upstairs think it's a gang thing," Detective Sarah Laine replied.

Nick looked up at his former partner. "Really?"

Sarah nodded grimly. "Problem is, nobody can come up with the suspect, even though there were, like, ten witnesses."

Nick picked up the case report. "Victim died of blood loss," he read, "Happened right after choir practice . . . Witnesses described a child assailant . . . Well, that's gruesome."

"Tell me about it," Sarah nodded. "But . . . "

"What?" Nick peered at her. "Is there something else?"

Sarah sighed. "Here's the thing," she began, glancing over the wall of Nick's cubicle to make sure there were no curious ears nearby. Nick could have told her that she didn't need to worry. Nobody in the basement offices of the downtown Seattle police station arrived until after sundown. To say that the officers who chose desks down here worked the night shift was all too accurate. Nick was an exception: At the time that he'd chosen a basement desk, his other options had been reassignment to the traffic division, or dismissal from the force.

"We found fibers on the victim," Sarah continued. "Hair. So we ran the DNA..."

"And?" Nick felt his pulse picking up speed. This was like arriving at a giant lake after crawling across a desert for months.

"Well, there was a match," Sarah lowered her voice even further. "But it's not that simple: You know how we've been running DNA on our cold case archives, right?"

"This is going to be good," said Nick.

Sarah nodded. "Good if you like *weird*. The hair fibers found on this victim, they match samples from a missing person's case, but not of the kidnapper — of the kidnapping *victim*. He was kidnapped as an infant. The hair fibers were from his stroller."

"Wow." Nick sat back. "So a kidnapped kid grew up to be a murderer —"

"But," Sarah continued, "The witnesses said a *child* did this. That kidnapping case was over sixty years ago. If this really is the same person, he'd be an old man by now, right?"

Nick didn't answer this. He gnawed on the well-chewed cap of his pen. "What about the parents of the missing kid?"

"They were killed at the scene. Christmas Eve, no less."

"So," Nick scanned the photos again. "Either your DNA results are wrong, or your witnesses are wrong. Or . . . " Nick eyed her. "You think there might be another answer. And that's why you brought this to me."

Sarah looked at him hopefully. "Any ideas you have, Nick . . . We're running dry upstairs, and this case is way public. It's been huge in the news. The families of the witnesses . . . They're all over us to find whatever — I mean, whoever did this."

Nick nodded. "I'll see what I can do. It was good to see you, Sarah."

"You too, partner," Sarah said with her smart smile. Nick had forgotten how much he missed it. She gave him a casual salute, then walked out.

Nick sat back. His face was lit by a tiny trapezoid of February sunlight, coming through the only window in the basement, right above his desk. For the past year, since Nick's demotion to the basement, he'd spent many long hours asleep in this little sliver of sun, feet up on the nearby radiator, thinking about how ironic it was that what he'd been demoted *for* had everything to do with why the other cops down here worked at night, why the one desk in the basement that got any sunlight was unoccupied, and why gruesome crimes like this Dean Aunders murder too often went unsolved in this town.

You know what did this he thought, running his finger over the photo of red holes in a young neck. *And you know you should just leave it alone. It'll only get you into more trouble that you don't want.*

But if there was one thing Nick had learned, it was that there wasn't the trouble that you wanted and the trouble you didn't. There was only the trouble you had. And here he was, with this trouble, once again.

Nick thumbed through the case file, reading the witness testimonies: *He looked our age; Wearing black; There were three other older kids; Really strong; It was like they could jump really far.* He felt a rush of adrenaline he hadn't felt in too long, except . . . it was worrisome. This connection — the missing child, the young killer, the events both so close to Christmas — It wasn't much to go on, but it did beg the question: Was this *him*? Could it possibly be?

Nick picked up the phone and dialed. "Hey, it's me," he said softly. "You won't believe this, but, I think I have a lead. . . . Yeah, it might be the one you've been looking for."

WHEN THE GATES BEGIN TO OPEN, THE MYSTERY UNFOLDS...